Introduction

According to Wikipedia "A dream is a succession of images, ideas, emotions, and sensations that usually occur involuntarily in the mind during certain stages of sleep. The content and purpose of dreams are not fully understood, although they have been a topic of scientific, philosophical and religious interest throughout recorded history. Dream interpretation is the attempt at drawing meaning from dreams and searching for an underlying message." Dreams can be completely forgotten in the morning, leaving either a fretful or soothing state of mind. However, dreams can also be etched in the memory of the morning and can be chronicled. This story is about the series of dreams by an interesting individual regarding a subject that is completely foreign to the individual's history. Over a period of several weeks, an octogenarian, Richard A. Weaver, experienced a mini-series of evening dreams regarding a story that needs to be told. His recall of the story, the players, the geography, the emotions and the dialogues are truly amazing as you will see on the ensuing pages.

Mr. Weaver is a resident of Florida with a plethora of life experiences. As a dyslectic, his early childhood was subject to criticism due to his inability to excel in school studies. His condition, undiagnosed at that time, led him to compensate by hard work and self-depreciating humor. Growing up in Glens Falls, New York, Mr. Weaver began working as a soda jerk at age 13. His diligent work efforts led him to another restaurant job, with the attendant 100% salary increase from $.50 to $1.00. Falling in love with his ninth-grade sweetheart, upon graduation from high school in 1950, he joined the Air Force then married his childhood darling. Stationed in Biloxi along with 60,000 servicemen, Mr. Weaver was trained in electronic fundamentals. He returned to New York following his service to utilize his electronic skills, joining NY Telephone. After eight years in Watertown, he decided to open a drive-in restaurant. The venture only lasted a year, though successful, a conflict with both his restaurant's landlord and NY Telephone led him to quit both ventures. As he went home to explain the situation with his wife, she said she wanted to move to Florida and enjoy the sun. Soon after the move she had a son to enjoy. Over the ensuing years his career took varied forms as he would blunder into different businesses that he would talk former owners into selling. In the meantime, he found time to father seven children. To illustrate his quick wit, during the fourth child's pregnancy, his mother was telling his wife what to do in preparation of the birth. To support his miffed wife, he once bellowed to his mother, "Mom, shut up about the baby, this one is not even mine!"

Mr. Weaver ended up in the small community of New Smyrna Beach, Florida. There he bought into a used furniture company that was successful in supplying the home ownership growth occurring in that section of Florida. That led to his meeting of another individual who was interested in selling his mill working business. This too, was successful as the demand for cabinetry matched that of the migration of tourists and retirees into the warm climate of central Florida. Once again, fate presented Weaver with another opportunity as his wife's real estate business was contracted to sell a sea shell company's resources. Now shell is an important building material in Florida as it one of the few places in the world that has virtually no native rock. Weaver recognized the opportunity and purchased the business. Not only did Weaver sell the shell, as he dug out the material, he created a quarry-like 73-acre lake. Around the clear waters of the white shell lake, he developed an upscale housing community that today is surrounded by million-dollar homes.

Truly, Mr. Weaver is a success by any measurement – his children are all well-educated and accomplished, he is financially secure and well liked and positioned within the community. In addition, given his dream recollections, he must be terribly intelligent. According to a study conducted by Cambridge Brain Sciences, "there is a deep connection between these particular squiggles of brain activity during sleep and 'fluid intelligence' as measured by high reasoning ability." Furthermore, a research study in 2017 discovered that "significant dream recall is linked to higher activity toward the front portion of the brain. The pre-frontal cortex is the part of the brain that deals with abstract thinking, so it makes sense that it has been linked to dream recall and lucid dreaming." Probably at this point it should be noted that Mr. Weaver is an accomplished, and self-taught, hypnotist who has used those skills to the betterment of people in pain. To compensate for his dyslexia, he has developed strong memory skills which may account for the extraordinary chronology of these dream events. Furthermore, his active mind and spirit have led him to a variety of entrepreneurial endeavors. Perhaps it is Mr. Weaver's unique set of personal skills and experiences which allowed him to build a sleep story about people he never knew, a place he had never been and circumstances that are completely foreign to his history. Certainly, Mr. Weaver is a unique individual and his dream story will keep you up at night.

Since this dream saga has no names, only vague geographical references and little dialogue, we have added these modest accommodations to assist the reader. The basic story is as Mr. Weaver recants in the chronical order in which his dreams captured his sleep. Each chapter is a separate dream that occurred on a different evening. Since, in the beginning, he had no idea that his initial dream would continue into a building story, it is remarkable that all the series were remembered, not just in the morning, but over a period of weeks. Nothing was written down and he had no idea when another piece of the puzzle would occur or if there would be an ending. And what an ending was in store for Mr. Weaver and for you!

Prologue

For the past half hour, he was watching the young lady climb. She had been arduously making her way up the mountainside completely unaware that she was being followed. He knew, however, and was waiting and watching. He knew he was invisible to both the hunters and the hunted. The skill of being unseen had served him well all his life and he had no fear of being seen now. His strength was in concealment and patience.

She was a memory to him. She had been there when he was abandoned. He was too young to keep up with his pack when they were pushed out of their hunting grounds by another group of the great greys. The lady had found him starving and exhausted and had taken him to her house. He was terrified of being separated from his pack and the strange surroundings that were the land of the humans. However, the lady nursed him back to health until she felt he was strong enough to survive on his own. When that day arrived, she took him back to the mountains and released him into the wild again.

Without a pack, he was a lone wolf. While his family had hunted by chasing and overpowering their prey. Their strength was the interdependence of the pack, the speed of the chase. He had learned to wait and watch. He found that by patience and stealth he could feed and fend for himself. He had become strong and healthy by relying on what he had learned. Instead of trying to run down his prey, he found that it was more prudent to use stealth and conserve his strength for the kill. He was a survivor. And he was invisible.

His attention turned to the two men that were following the lady. They stayed a distance from her but slowly climbed side by side. Sometimes they would even talk together. He recognized that they were not good hunters but were still a threat to the lady who had saved his life. After their last conversation, they began to speed up and it was apparent they were closing in on the unsuspecting lady. Just like his pack chased their prey, the two men were moving quickly with the malice of hunters anticipating the kill. It was then that he decided to attack.

The lady turned when she heard the growls and subsequent scream of the first man that the wolf pounced upon. The hundred and fifty pounds of canine fury knocked the man on the ground and his revealed throat made a quick death to the hunter. Before the second human could react with a weapon, the lone wolf turned on him. Snarling and slashing on the second man's wrist, with his weapon dropped, the man was an easy target for the powerful jaws. The man tried to escape but backed into a crevasse and fell to his death.

Daniel didn't know if it was the screams of the falling man or his own that woke him from his nightmare. He was only twelve and, in an instant his sister was by his side to comfort him. He had never had a nightmare so real and so frightening. Little was he to know just how possible that dreams can become reality and that his future would be shaped by nocturnal visitations.

Chapter 1 My First Dream

Unlike Kafka's Gregor Samsa, I did not awaken from a fitful dream to find myself transformed into some monstrous vermin. However, as I awoke, I was mindful that I had experienced a dream that seemed so real, so unforgettable that all the various details were glued into my memory. As I explained the dream to my wife at breakfast, I was at a loss as to how to describe how explicit it seemed. While there was no conclusion to this nocturnal story, the portion I could recall was as vivid as watching a movie. Two nights later, the tale continued exactly where I remember it ended from the first dream. What a shock to awaken with a new chapter to my story. Night after night it became a saga that built upon itself in subsequent dreams in such continuity that I was frightened that it would never end. I was, however, equally fearful that there would be no ending and the story would leave me forever at a loss of closure. Here is the story of my dreams.

He was borne at the outset of the great foreign war he never heard of, in a log cabin just north of Kaak, Montana. His parents named their only son Daniel simply because his father's father had read of the bold exploits of the famous explorer Daniel Boone. It sounded like a strong name. Daniel's father spent his time trapping, hunting and a little panning for the gold that washed downstream from the Kootenai

Falls. Daniel's mother was pure Blackfoot Indian who met her husband on a trading journey from her native British Columbia. From early on, Daniel's father instilled within his son a strong sense of respect for the outdoors and honor among its human and otherwise inhabitants. From his mother, Daniel developed a charming personality, strikingly high cheekbones, black hair and good looks. Daniel was also blessed with an older sister Sarah who doted on him and assisted with his education. As Kaak was little more than what could be classified as a 'settlement', schooling was only available from family and the infrequent circuit of a preacher who doubled as an educator. Sarah was a natural in the understanding of mathematics and pushed Daniel's knowledge of the tables and formulas of figures. Life of the 1940's in northernmost Montana was harsh and lonely. In this isolated part of the world, however, ignorance of the lifestyles of others was bliss. Conversely, the fears associated with the war on foreign soil were not on the radar of Daniel's family. They had each other and they all possessed the power of self-reliance.

As Daniel grew, as with all children, he began to develop his own personality. On his eighth birthday, his parents gave him a little crystal radio with an attached earpiece. He could barely hear stations that were as far away as Kalispell and Cranbrook, but they became a window to a different world, far away from the isolation of Kaak. For some reason each night the radio signals were stronger than during the day. That was fine with Daniel as he had plenty to do during the daylight hours. However, he would stay up late to hear of local and world news, sports, music and stories. While some children would use a flashlight to devour books under their covers, Daniel would escape into real worlds brought to him through the little radio. It was from this window in his earpiece that he began to look outside his harsh world and into the realm of sunshine and luxury.

Many summer evenings Daniel and Sarah would sit on the front porch of the little cabin and watch the lightning bugs come out. With their yellow beacons flashing across the black Montana sky they made a path of light as they sought mates. Sarah would tell Daniel that they were very lucky to see them because lightning bugs were rare in Montana and, indeed, throughout the West.

"They seem so random with their flight and the time that they crank up their lights," Daniel asked.

"Well, I like to think that they are wanderers always looking for something that only each one of them knows. Maybe, they are a little like people. Some people like to stay at home where it is safe and familiar. Others like to experience new things, new places and new adventures. Mother and Father prefer the simple life up here where they have made a home and raised us as a family. This is their choice in life, and they are happy with it. Perhaps, there are lightening bugs that stay on the ground where they feel secure. We cannot see them because they need not turn on their light. Others, however, chart a different course as they take flight and send out their beacons." Spoke Sarah.

"When I grow up, I want to be like the lightening bugs that shine. Remember when we had a jar and caught a bunch of them as they flew, and they made that jar as bright as lamp. It was so much fun to catch them and watch them in the jar. I wonder how they make their tails such a pretty and bright yellow color." Daniel responded.

"I don't know how they do it nor do I know why." Sarah said.

"I know!" Daniel exclaimed in his attempt at a grown-up voice. "The wanderers have such a strong will that they grit their teeth so hard that the friction causes them to glow. Remember when I run with you playing hide and seek. If I run very fast to get to the base, I feel really hot and my face turns red. I bet it is just like the lightening bugs only they turn yellow."

"Well, that is certainly a possibility. But just like the lightening bugs, what do you want to do with your life? You can be safe here with our little family or will you choose to be a wanderer like the lightening bugs? Some day you will make a choice as to what makes you happy. Life is full of choices that you will have to make. Chose them wisely but use your skills, upbringing, and love to help make the right direction for you."

Daniel was happy growing up in Kaak where he assisted his family in their simple quest for daily survival. He never felt underprivileged because everyone he knew had the same lifestyle. They worked hard, relied upon their family and neighbors but prayed that they could avoid accidents and illness. Any form of setback from their daily routine would be costly. Therefore, even at such a young age, Daniel was trained and expected to serve as a backup should anything happen to his father. The reliance upon him by the family built a sense of confidence and inner strength that seldom comes at such a young age. There was something in his DNA that made him special. His mother was the daughter of a chief of a tribe within the Blackfoot Nation. His father's father was a wealthy vagabond who was variously purported to be a sailor, a miner, a gambler, drinker and a man to avoid when roused. The descriptions were probably all true. The combination of genetic histories left Daniel with a sharp mind, watchful eye, an overburdened since of loyalty and an itch to be more than he could be in Kaak. There was truly something 'special' about

Daniel and he always felt that his destiny was to exploit those traits. Maybe he would be like the lightening bugs.

His wanderlust was fueled each night as he heard tales about the great cities of the Pacific Northwest. He wanted to see the things he was only able to hear about. One thing was perfectly clear, to enjoy the life outside Kaak and to fulfill his destiny, money would be needed and his only hope of gaining his spot in the sun would be through gold. His father's hunting and trapping put food on the table, but it was his meager gold findings that brought in the ability to purchase items at the county trading post. Gold was the answer if Daniel ever wished to live the life he had only heard about. By no way was Daniel greedy or covetous. He lived by the respect and honor that his family taught him. He was merely ambitious to see the world that was unfolding to him through his crystal radio each evening.

To underscore the character that was developing within the young Daniel, there was an incident that involved the travelling preacher. While staying with Daniel's family, the preacher suddenly became ill and needed digitalis for his heart condition. With no ready source for the drug and Daniel's father running the trap line, it was Daniel's responsibility to hike some fifteen miles to the nearest pharmacy. Knowing the gravity of the situation, Daniel trekked his way through the forest in record time. On the return, however, darkness was starting to fall and the twelve-year-old became anxious over his situation. He knew of the dangers in the forest but also knew that he had a duty to perform. While the great grizzly bear was foremost of his fears, mountain lions, wolves and falling were threats that came with the darkening forest. Fortunately, there was little chance that he would become lost since all he had to do was to follow the Kaak River northward toward home. In that period between the fall of the sun on the horizon and the rising of the moon, he heard the yipping of a pack of wolves to his south. They appeared to be on the East side of the river, but Daniel knew that there were some shallows that could allow a crossing to his side. Daniel had seen the power of a pack of the great grey wolves as they once killed a mature elk when he was on the trap line with his father. He knew he would have no chance if he was caught by a hungry pack that has no fear of mankind. Suddenly, he could hear paws splashing in the shallows behind him. Just as he was looking for a tree, he could quickly climb, he heard the report of a rifle and saw his father just ahead. As the greys melted back into the shadows, Daniel's father and he marched onward to their cabin.

The preacher's condition had worsened during the day, but he responded well to the digitalis. In the morning he felt well enough to continue his circuit

but, in his profound gratitude, he presented young
Daniel with the first book he was ever to own. This
book provided Daniel with yet another window to
the outside world. Complete with photographs, the
book was a travel primer on the emerald city of the
west - Vancouver. Hour after hour, Daniel would
look at all the pictures of homes and streets and
parks with their orderly gardens of flowers. He could
see the clothes the people wore and the cars they
drove. The great buildings of the city invoked
amazement and the ornate facades of banks made
him wonder about how it would be to work in such
a place. He spoke at length with his parents and
Sarah about his desire to experience a life away from
Kaak. While his sister and mother encouraged the
young lad to follow his dream, his father worried
about the family if something should happen to him
with Daniel not there. As time went by, Daniel grew
into a strong and handsome man with excellent
verbal skills thanks to his nightly radio worship. The
day following Daniel's nineteenth birthday, Sarah
was married to a young man in the settlement. He
was quite a skilled provider and committed to the
Kaak life. His infusion into the family thus provided
Daniel with the answer to his father's concerns.

A year later, Daniel kissed his family goodbye and
headed to Vancouver and the life that he had so long
dreamed of experiencing. The first evening away
from home he spotted a sole lightening bug. It flew

in the general direction Daniel was headed and
caused Daniel to reflect on that long-ago discussion
with Sarah about wanderers and what life course he
would take. He took the vision as a good omen that
he had made the right choice. After two days on the
road he made it as far as Trail, British Columbia
where he stopped to try and replenish his meager
supply of cash. With several thousand residents,
Trail was a big city in Daniel's eyes. He believed he
could settle there for a few weeks doing odd jobs
and earning the incremental capital needed for the
remainder of the trip. One evening after a hard day
of chopping wood for a widow and her lovely
daughter, he decided to treat himself to a meal in the
local diner. It was there that he met a man that
would change his life forever.

Daniel sat down in the town's only restaurant not
sure of what his future held. He didn't know where
he would spend the night, how to order from a
menu, if his shabby clothes would serve to
embarrass or shun him from the townspeople or
even if his daily wage would be enough to cover the
cost of his meal. Clearly, he looked out of place even
though Trail had its share of frontier characters.

As he discussed the food offerings with the waitress,
a kindly gentleman asked if he could be of assistance.
Always respectful of elders, Daniel gratefully
accepted the assistance and, with his help, ordered

spaghetti, the cheapest thing on the menu. Since Daniel had never even heard of spaghetti, he was apprehensive of what he might be eating. Mr. Truesdale explained that it was a thin pasta with tomato and spicy sauce, sometimes with meat or sausage, however, that would be more expensive. Daniel opted for just the tomato sauce. Mr. Truesdale found Daniel interesting in his naivete when compared to his manners, demeanor and good looks.

Mr. Truesdale was a giant, but not in stature. In fact, he was a rather smallish man with a groomed gray beard, little hands and with sky blue eyes that implied a Celtic or Nordic family history. He was, however, a man that carried himself with the supreme self-confidence that education, experience and success provide. As they say out west and in the southern states, the man has a 'presence'. When he walked into a room he was immediately noticed and respected. It was that air about him that commanded attention and when he spoke, the room silenced to his authority. He was quite jovial and preferred to use humor rather than dogmatism to present his case. He was sympathetic to others and built lasting friendships, as he was always the first to assist others in time of crisis. He was a man for all seasons. He was the 'man' that Rudyard Kipling envisioned in his famous poem 'If'.

In conversation, Daniel discussed his goal of going to Vancouver and finding employment there. He explained his past circumstances and how he believed his future destiny was out of Kaak and into the big city. Mr. Truesdale warned him that the big city also presented big problems but empathized with Daniel's desires to see a different world. The two became immersed in conversation as each discovered the other's past. There were similarities and differences but the two got along well. As Daniel explained he was seeking some part-time employment in Trail, Truesdale told him he needed to gain some form of identification and should go to the local Mounties office in the morning. He asked Daniel if he had a place to stay the evening. Daniel remarked that he would just pitch a tent in a park he saw near the widow's home. Truesdale said that would be illegal and probably not the best way to meet the Mounties in the morning. Truesdale suggested he could spend the night in his home just down the street. With a bit of a tear in his eye, he told Daniel that he had lost his only son in the war and would be happy to have Daniel use the son's room that evening. Before they left the diner, Truesdale suggested that Daniel leave a bit extra for the waitress. This confused Daniel but did as the elder suggested. Perhaps his smile and good looks would be sufficient for the waitress, but as Daniel was becoming aware, cash is king!

At the Truesdale home he was viewed with a wary eye by Mrs. Truesdale. Mr. Truesdale was not accustomed to bringing home guests that were strangers to the community. Nevertheless, she welcomed him and showed him to their son's quarters. Daniel had never seen such a home. He marveled at all the electric lights, the wallpaper, the fancy furnishings and rugs. The thing that really caught his eye, however, was the television set. Certainly, he had heard of their existence but had never seen a picture that could move inside a box. He was mesmerized but minded his manners and headed off to his room. In the room Daniel was shocked to see there was an indoor bathroom complete with shower. The walls of the room had pennants and various athletic gear and pictures of sports heroes. The bed was of two sections, one with springs and the other with soft cushioning and covered with sheets and blankets. He was used to a single hard mattress over a grid of leather straps. Daniel cleaned up and climbed into bed but was having difficulty sleeping as his excitement over the day's revelations spun in his mind. He finally slept and had a dream about his parents and sister back in Kaak. When he awoke, he felt a little homesick and missed seeing the faces that he had seen every day of his life. He prayed that he had made the right decision and that he hadn't forsaken his family to pursue his selfish dreams.

He could smell coffee brewing and bacon frying, so he quickly dressed and made up the bed as he recalled its appearance before he slept in it the night before. He wandered out of his room and nearly crashed into Mr. Truesdale who was already dressed in a suit and tie. He beckoned Daniel to join him for breakfast before he went to the bank and Daniel went to meet the Mounties. At breakfast Truesdale explained how to find the Mounties' station and how best to approach them with his situation. He said that if Daniel had any problems with the law authorities, he should use Mr. Truesdale's name and that should 'grease the skids'. He also asked Daniel to come by the bank around lunchtime and he would possibly find some work for Daniel to do in the office. Other than game wardens, Daniel had little experience with the police and certainly didn't have any concept of the bureaucracy of government. Neither did he know what 'grease the skids' meant but was prepared to do it if he was in trouble.

He was greeted at the door of the Mounties' office by Sergeant Bigsby. Dressed in his red and black uniform with three stripes and a crown on top, Sergeant Bigsby exuded a superiority countenance. The sergeant was a rather average looking fellow that seemed completely indifferent to Daniel but pointed to a chair in the office waiting room. Daniel sat down and started looking for any skids that needed greasing. About twenty minutes later another similarly dressed fellow came in and introduced himself as Superintendent Felps. In a few words, Daniel relayed the fact that he had come in from Montana looking for work. Since he had no identification whatsoever, Felps was skeptical of this rugged looking stranger who admitted he crossed into Canada illegally. He immediately got on the phone to 'regional headquarters to seek some guidance as to what to do. After a lot of shaking of his head, he finally hung up and brought Daniel into a separate room. He explained that unless Daniel wanted to apply for citizenship and pay formidable fees, he should just return to Kaak. Daniel tried to argue with the superintendent but to no avail until he mentioned that his mother was from a Blackfoot tribe in Canada. Felps again called 'regional headquarters' and explained the newly discovered circumstances. Again, after considerable nodding and coughing, he hung up and told Daniel would still have to apply for citizenship although fees would be waived. Daniel couldn't understand why all the fuss over a piece of paper, but it was when he explained that he had to leave to have lunch with Mr. Truesdale, the skids became greased. "So, how do you know Mr. Truesdale?" asked the superintendent. Daniel mentioned he was a house guest and was to meet that afternoon about employment. Now, while the Mounties purportedly 'always get their man', they invariably predetermine which man they want to get. Some they decide are better left alone. This became the case with Daniel and his greasy-skid friend Mr. Truesdale.

Daniel had been given the address of the Truesdale Bank and Trust and showed up at the front façade at exactly noon. The receptionist buzzed Mr. Truesdale who greeted Daniel like an old friend. The bank looked nothing like in the book that had spawned his dreams of the big city. The building was brick and substantial looking. It did not, however, have the marble façade and the great fluted columns that he remembered from pictures. Inside, the floor was industrial terrazzo and the walls simply painted a government shade of green. There was little in the way of adornments on the walls and the furniture was simple wood. There was a fortress-like wall of tellers that were constantly busy with dealing with customers. Clearly, there were favorites among the tellers as certain customers queued up in lines of their choice. Communication between clients and tellers was conducted in whispers as, in most small towns, everyone knows everything about each other.

The twosome walked to the same diner as last evening and enjoyed a soup and sandwich with Truesdale picking up the tab. Daniel recounted his discussions with the Mounties and Truesdale said he would run by and see if the citizenship issue could be conducted through the mail instead of making that superfluous trip to Mountie Headquarters. Futhermore, Mr. Truesdale indicated that there was a need for some assistance in the teller line of the bank. He asked Daniel if he was any good at math. Daniel was proud to tell him that his sister had a predisposition for mathematics and had been a good mentor in that part of his schooling.

As they were enjoying their meal, the widow's daughter walked in with a friend. Daniel was immediately smitten with the young lady's companion and couldn't help himself by both staring and smiling. The widow's daughter stopped by the table and introduced Tess to Daniel. Daniel stood and offered his hand but was so tongue-tied that he could hardly speak. Mr. Truesdale, once again, came to the rescue and carried the brief conversation until Daniel could blurt out how pleased he was to meet her. Tess told them that she was home from school in the East and would summer in Trail until she entered college in the fall. Her parents always summer at a rental cottage in Trail which is how she had developed the friendship with the widow's daughter. She explained that she was looking forward to doing some hiking and relaxing before heading to school in the States.

Daniel's bubble burst as Sergeant Bigsby strolled into the diner and spoke to the widow's daughter in a familiar fashion. Clearly, there was some connection there, but he seemed more interested in Tess. Tess appeared flattered by the Mountie's attention, although Daniel failed to see why a beauty like Tess would be attracted to someone like Bigsby. He didn't understand the power a sharp uniform has over impressionable young ladies. Nonetheless, they said their goodbyes and the girls sat with the sergeant and had their lunch. Daniel did notice that Tess would make eye contact with him every so often during the meal, so he felt all was not lost. Unfortunately, Bigsby also noticed the 'across the room' flirtation and would scowl at Daniel whenever the girls weren't looking.

Dream Two

Tess was initially intrigued by the older Sergeant across from her in the crisp Mountie uniform. He was not all that handsome, but something about his authority, experiences and bumbling pattern of speaking were of certain interest. The more he talked, however, the less intrigued she became. He would start a story about chasing after bad guys but wouldn't be able to articulate the timing of the event or outcome in much of a cohesive fashion. She began to feel he was 'manufacturing' the story and his brain couldn't keep up with how he hoped to end it in such a fashion as to impress the girls. He would ramble off saying how he single-handedly captured two cattle thieves but couldn't explain how he managed to bring both the cattle and the two perpetrators back to Trail.

On the other hand, the handsome and mannerly young stranger who was clearly flirting with her from across the room, had seemed so honest and open. He was incredibly handsome and quite the physical specimen, however seemed to not recognize his attributes. The fact that his background was so different from her own only added to the appeal. She was a city girl with impressive social and educational experiences. He was of a humble background, however, despite the lack of refinery in his upbringing, he seemed to possess values that led to his character. Tess had a feeling that she would like to know this humble hulk better.

"And that's why they say that the Mounties always get their man," Bigsby ended his story.

Tess's mind had been wandering and had missed his whole dialogue. All she could muster was a meek, "Oh".

"Yes, it isn't easy being the law in these parts. Those big city Mounties think they are so much smarter than us bumpkins in the territories. Me and the Superintendent have had to deal with all kinds of criminals and we always get our man!"

Ok, you don't have to knock me in the head with the 'always get our man' talk, thought Tess. She was becoming completely bored with Bixby and his showing off.

"Well, I must be going. I must pick up Mom and Dad at the train station. They are coming in this afternoon and I need to stock the house with groceries."

"I would be happy to help you," exclaimed the Sergeant. "I don't have any pressing issues this afternoon".

"Thanks, but no, I like to take my time at the grocers and have some other errands to run." She exclaimed, however she thought but didn't say, 'don't you have to go get your man'.

"Thank you for lunch Sergeant Bigsby," stated Tess and to her companion, "Will you come over sometime this week for dinner? I'm sure Mom and Dad would love to catch up with you and hear your summer plans."

After saying her good-byes, Tess strolled by the booth where Daniel and Mr. Truesdale were finishing their lunch. She gently touched Daniel's hand and said how delighted she was to have met them both and how she hoped to see them again. Truesdale could sense the budding chemistry between the two and suggested they have lunch together with her parents. The wily old banker thought he could kill two birds with one stone. He could help his young new employee and, at the same time, meet some likely depositors to his bank.

"I would very much like that," expressed Tess, "how can I get in touch with you?"

Mr. Truesdale gave her his telephone number at home and at the bank as well. "Call me anytime and we can make arrangements." He smiled as he relished his 'matchmaker' role.

Across the room Bigsby was monitoring the dialogue between the beauty and the stranger. He was not happy with her dismissal of his 'shopping' offer and the obvious chemistry between Tess and Daniel. He was determined that the stranger needed to leave Trail and he would find a way to make that happen.

"Well, let's get back to the office," exclaimed Truesdale after Tess left their table. "She's quite a good look and I hear that her family is quite respectable. They summer here and her father used to be a bit of a frontiersman like yourself before he moved to the city. I understand he made a good living as a commodities broker. Seems I heard he specialized in gold trading between some of the big Canadian mines and India."

The mention of gold snapped Daniel out of his thoughts of Tess and how he hoped to meet her again.

"I would love to ask him about that business. My dad used to pan for gold and was able to get some out of the streams. He never made much because it seemed all the profit went to the assayer and traders like Tess's dad."

"That is the way of business, my young friend," said Truesdale. "It happens with farmers and lumbermen. They do the hard work and the people with trade connections reap the major profits."

They went back to the bank and Truesdale introduced Daniel to the ladies in the teller line and asked him to watch them and learn a bit about what they do. The tellers were excited to have the cute boy working with them and they eagerly showed him their various procedures and how to deal with customers. They also explained how different their role within the services of the bank was with that of the lending function. The lending staff had all the prestige because loans were the income engine of the bank and tellers dealt with deposits, which are liabilities of the company. He took notes and asked questions whenever there was a lull in the customer line.

Once, a teller was asked to assist a client with conversion from U.S. currency into Canadian dollars. Daniel was watching as the teller was having difficulty with the math. Daniel immediately calculated the conversion ratio for the transaction in his mind and wrote it down and handed it to the teller. The customer was impressed with the ease and confidence that Daniel had handled the complex procedure. Likewise, the teller was pleased to have his support and how he handled the communication to her in such a professional fashion. Little did Daniel know that the customer would soon be introduced to him under totally different circumstances.

At the end of the day, Mr. Truesdale and Daniel walked back to the Truesdale home. By now he had gained the trust and confidence of Mrs. Truesdale who welcomed them both and asked about their day.

"Well," returned Mr. Truesdale, "Daniel comported himself well on the teller line. I had a new customer come to my office and compliment him on a currency transaction. Seems our young friend here has also caught the eye of a lovely young lady during lunch. Her family is well known in the city and they are spending the summer here. I invited them to lunch with us. What do you think about sometime this weekend?"

"Well, if it will further any budding romance in this dreary town, I am all for it." Lady Truesdale exclaimed. "We could use a little intrigue around here and some new gossip would certainly set the quilting bees a-buzzing."

Through all these discussions, Daniel's complexion was cast in a variety of shades of pink until the word 'romance' turned him into a shocking bright red. He had just arrived into town, had the great fortune to meet a man that was bringing him unexpected kindness in a variety of fronts, had a stressful meeting with the law authorities, met a beautiful young woman and, if Mrs. Truesdale is accurate, will become the talk of the town. It was as if the moon traded shifts with the sun and he was overwhelmed.

Daniel begged off dinner and asked if he could go to bed. The day had provided many new experiences and he wanted to replay them in his mind. Just as the crystal radio had, every evening in Kaak, provided him a window to the outside world, the night was his place of peace and dreams. He wanted to relive every moment of his work and the beguiling young woman he had just met. He fell asleep trying to recall every feature of Tess's face, the outline of her cheekbones, her pouty nose and the perpetual smile that highlighted perfectly white teeth. He awoke, startled from a nightmare wherein Sergeant Bigsby kept pushing him down the street, shouting, "She's mine, American, go back to Montana, we don't want your kind in our town." While the flood of relief that this was just a dream caused Daniel to sigh, he could still feel the knots in his stomach and hear his heart racing. Instinctively, he knew that this dream was a warning and a precursor of issues he might face if he stayed long in Trail.

Having had no dinner, Daniel was ravenous at breakfast but minded his manners and chatted with Mrs. Truesdale. When Mr. Truesdale came down, he smiled a knowing little grin at Daniel. "Well, my boy, you shouldn't have gone off to bed so early last night. You missed a nice telephone conversation I had with that lovely young lady Tess. She called and suggested we make plans for lunch. Her parents were eager to discuss some financial issues in which the bank might be of assistance, so we set something up for Saturday lunch here at the house. However, Tess seemed a bit disappointed that I had answered the phone!" he winked at Mrs. Truesdale. "I hope you haven't made other plans for the weekend?"

"No, no sir, I would be more than happy to have lunch with the most beautiful girl in Canada! Pretty sure I can fit it into my schedule."

His excitement, however, turned to terror as he realized he had no good clothes or shoes and he certainly was not versed in the proper handling of cutlery and other fineries of high society. Mr. Truesdale, ever the perceptive savant, could almost read Daniel's mind and, once again, proved to provide the answer to every dilemma.

"What if I upfronted you your first week's salary and we run up town to buy you some new clothes?"

Daniel looked embarrassed as he said, "Thank you Mr. Truesdale but it's not just clothes I'm worried about, I don't know what to say, when to eat what and which silverware to use. I don't want to embarrass you or myself!"

Mrs. Truesdale chimed in, "Don't you fret one tiny bit, honey, I will have you set to meet the Queen herself by the time this weekend arrives! I saw that play Pygmalion down at the Royal Theatre on Bay

Avenue and I learned every trick in the book about etiquette training."

"Well, if you are willing to teach me, I'm willing to learn - but now I better head down to the bank and start earning my keep."

Daniel and Mr. Truesdale walked to the office and discussed some of the particulars of banking. Daniel was particularly interested in the mathematics behind the role of interest rates on deposit gathering and making of loans. He was thankful that Mr. Truesdale was so patient with him in explaining what was elementary to him but a mystery to Daniel.

"I want you to work with Sylvia, our head teller today and see if you can devise a formula that all the staff can use in that currency conversion you tackled yesterday. I heard nothing but praise from the teller crew so keep it up…they can turn on you like a wolverine in a leg trap. Don't piss them off!"

Daniel worked hard in the ensuing days and was particularly attentive to the tellers and the customers in which he came into contact. However, after days of working at the bank and being cooped up inside, Daniel was eager to be outside. His whole life had been associated with the outdoors and it was taking all his discipline to stay within four walls. He spent all his lunches in the park across the street from the bank. There was a gazebo where he would unwrap the sandwiches and usually a Nanaimo bar which Mrs. Truesdale packed for him. Mrs. Truesdale had recently returned from a small city on Vancouver Island where she had learned about this cookless pastry. Daniel was not familiar with desserts on a consistent basis. In Kaak, his family only had sweets on special occasions except for the wild fruit that his mother would boil and can as preserves. Lunch was something Daniel looked forward to as he appreciated both the fresh air and Mrs. Truesdale's fine food. Once or twice during lunches he thought he saw Tess walking with the widow's daughter. She was too far away to tell for sure and he thought better of pursuing them. He would just have to wait until Saturday.

Mr. Truesdale had helped Daniel set up a checking account and made sure that all his paychecks would be deposited into the bank. Together they went shopping for clothes and, for the first time, Daniel was told not to buy clothes too big for himself. He had forgotten that he had stopped growing and, with finer clothes, shrinkage after washing wasn't like the clothes, he had in Kaak. He was starting to understand the differences, both subtle and obvious, between the frontier and the city. In the meantime, Mrs. Truesdale spent a lot of time with Daniel on etiquette and some of the proprieties of a more cultured life. With Tess in mind, he was dedicated in his studies and when Saturday arrived, he felt a bit more confident in himself.

Daniel spent early Saturday helping with chores around the house. He was so grateful for all that the Truesdale's had done for him he was always eager to try to return the favors. Prior to lunch, he found an hour to wash up, shave and trim his hair and put on his new clothes. The minutes before the noon hour seemed to creep by ever so slowly, adding to both his excitement and anxiety. He had always felt confident in his physicality and his general intelligence. However, it was his lack of worldliness that worried him the most. Certainly, Tess's family had traveled and experienced things that were far removed from the encounters of Daniel in his humble background. He doubted that his knowledge of how to hunt moose or set a wolf trap would be of much conversational interest.

Finally, Mr. Truesdale announced that their guests had arrived and for him to come downstairs and join them for lunch. As Daniel walked down the stairs his eyes first focused on Tess. He had not seen her with make-up and permed hair and was shocked that she was even prettier than when he had met her at the diner. Her smile when their eyes met was genuine and she blushed a bit, adding to her allure. Then, he recognized her father as the gentleman that he had helped with the currency translation on his first day on the job. That was something of a relief, since he had gotten good feedback from that experience and his efforts were appreciated. Tess's mother was very refined looking, and she and Tess could have been sisters instead of mother-daughter.

"How do you do," exclaimed Daniel as he took Tess's dad's hand. "I am very glad to meet you."

"Oh, let's just call it 'glad to see you again' since I recall having met you at the bank earlier this week." He explained to Tess and her mother that Daniel had assisted in some currency issues as they needed U.S. dollars converted into Canadian. He noted how impressed he was in the way Daniel had professionally handled the situation. Now it was Daniel's turn to blush a bit under the praise.

Certainly, young ladies learn at an early age that, in dealings with young men, they need to be both coy while remaining open and inviting. Tess was aware of her impact upon men of all ages. She was aware that she was attractive. From infancy through adolescence and into her teen years, people had constantly made over her good looks. While she felt her looks were from no effort on her part, just a fortunate circumstance of genetics, her pride came from her kindness and the intellect that emanated from her curious mind. When she walked into a room, eyes would turn to her just as they seemed to when Mr. Truesdale entered. Both had that undefinable 'presence' that transcended their good looks and gave them a certain dominance under any social occasion.

Mr. Truesdale made all the introductions and Tess's dad made sure that Daniel call him by his first name which was Gus. Gus was nothing like what Daniel was expecting. For some reason, Daniel thought that Tess's dad would be a lot like Mr. Truesdale. Refined and proper, reserved and circumspect. Instead, Gus was boisterous and bold. He had wide shoulders and muscled arms that barely fit into his shirt sleeves. As he had with Tess, Daniel felt an immediate bond with Gus.

With introductions complete, the five sat down to lunch. Mrs. Truesdale had prepared a sumptuous meal with smoked salmon, salad, tomato aspic and boiled potatoes. For dessert they had a cake that Daniel had never experienced or even heard about. It was made of some fruit that he had never tasted, and Mrs. Truesdale told him it was called a pineapple upside down cake. He couldn't figure out what was upside down but didn't want to ask. The conversation was carried by the Truesdale's as they welcomed Tess' family to Trail and told them about what was going on in the city. Mrs. Truesdale spoke to Tess and her mom about some new stores that had opened since last summer and how the theatre was carrying two new films. North by Northwest and Ben Hur were recent movies that had just arrived in Trail. Mr. Truesdale, ever the businessman, chatted with Gus on some banking issues and the economy. Daniel was quiet, taking it all in, but forced himself not to stare at Tess, although she spent a considerable amount of the lunch making quick glances at Daniel. She was excellent at her craft of being both coy and alluring. At some point, the discussions turned to gold and Gus explained how he got into the commodities business. He described how he had always had a fascination with gold ever since he had run a sluice line down in Montana.

"Mr. Truesdale tells me that you are from Montana." He asked Daniel.

"Yes sir, I grew up on the Kaak river just a bit north of town. My dad was a trapper and he would sometimes take me down to the Kootenai Falls to do some panning. He stopped taking me and, finally quit going himself because there were some bad men down there. He told stories of miners that had been robbed and, sometimes, even disappeared. It had become a dangerous place and dad had family responsibilities and couldn't afford to turn up dead over some small pieces of rock."

Gus asked Daniel, "What is your father's name?"

Daniel replied, which caused Gus to stand up and exclaim that Daniel's father was an old friend. "Now I see the resemblance. I thought you looked familiar when I first saw you at the bank! Your dad and I camped several times on the river and he was always a straight up guy. I hope he is doing well?"

"He is a happy man now that my sister has married and is staying in Kaak. He was always worried about our family and what might happen to them should he have an accident. Too many in his line of work have shortened careers or lives! I think he wishes that I had stayed but is happy about Sarah's marriage and remaining in Kaak."

"So, I guess you have enjoyed seeing your great aunt now that you have settled down in Trail?"

This time is was Daniel who jumped up from the table, "What relative are you talking about? I don't know anyone in town other than at the bank or the Truesdale's!"

Your father asked me to say hello to his mother's sister the next time I come to Trail. Unfortunately, I forgot about that just until you jogged my memory of your dad. Did he never tell you about your great aunt?"

"No, I think he had a falling out many years ago with his parents. I do recall that my sister Sarah had mentioned that we had some relatives in Canada. I had no idea that someone here in Trail might be kinfolk! Do you know her name?"

"I'll try to remember but can't recall just now. Maybe some of Mrs. Truesdale's pineapple upside cake and a cup of that coffee I smell might jog my memory."

The rest of the lunch was a delightful affair with plenty of conversations and furtive glances between the two budding love birds. At the meal's end Daniel offered to clear the table and wash the dishes. As he was starting his chore, Tess stood to help and the two carried the dishes and tableware into the kitchen. Daniel rolled up his sleeves and started running the faucet into the sink. Unfortunately, as stately and proper was Mrs. Truesdale in her personal appearance, she was a disaster in the kitchen. Pots and pans were all over the place and every utensil in the kitchen had been used and left in the exact spot when their usefulness was completed. Needless to say, an hour of washing and cleaning had created a new closeness between the couple. Daniel understood you never really know someone until you have poured some sweat together. His appreciation for Tess grew as she undertook the cleanup with a smile and with gusto. In fact, it became something of a contest between the two to see who could work the quickest. They had just started flipping soap suds on each other when Gus walked into the kitchen.

"Well, I remembered your great aunt's name. Mr. Truesdale knows her and is ringing her up right now. If I can break you away from this soap spatter contest, you might want to join him in the study."

Daniel excused himself and hurried into the study just as Mr. Truesdale was explaining the circumstances of the conversation. When he saw Daniel arrive, he said, "Elizabeth, here is young Daniel now, would you like to speak to him?"

He handed the phone to Daniel and explained that his great aunt Elizabeth was anxious to talk to him. With his hand over the phone's mouthpiece, he told Daniel, "Your great aunt Elizabeth is getting on in years and is a bit hard of hearing. You might want to speak up. She is a wonderful lady and a bellwether of the community."

"Hello, Aunt Elizabeth." Daniel said. "I am pleased to make your acquaintance. My father never spoke of his family much and I am stunned to find that I have a relative here in Trail. I hope this isn't presenting any difficulties for you."

"Don't be impertinent, young man. Of course, I am happy to hear from you and I would like to hear about your father. I hope he is well. I haven't heard anything from him for years but did understand that he and your mother had had a new baby boy. That was the last I had any word from him. He and your grandfather had a terrible falling out and both stubborn men refused to make amends or even discuss the nature of the dissolution of their relationship."

Daniel was at a loss of what to say, but didn't need to as Elizabeth continued, "Well, now, I am dying to meet you. Mr. Truesdale told me you were working with him at the bank, so I presume you are free tomorrow to escort me to church."

"Well, I would love that." Just as the words came out of his mouth Tess entered the room. Quickly, he added, "Would you mind if I asked someone to join us? I met a new friend here in Trail and don't have much free time to socialize."

"That would be fine. At my age, I love the company and I want you to catch me up on your life and what brought you to Trail. How about coming over around 10 for a cup of tea and some conversation before church service at 11:00? What is the name of your friend?"

Before he answered, he nodded to Tess and asked her if she would like to join the two for church. With an enthusiastic grin, she accepted the offer and Daniel spoke into the phone, "Tess is her name and her family is here for the summer before she goes away to college. I think she could use some gospel after spraying me with dishwater soap!"

Dream Three, Dream Inside a Dream

He awoke from some vague dream with a start. Something was wrong with his body. Wrong but not painful. In fact, his whole body was encountering some sensation which he had never felt before. It was almost as if he was being jolted by some invisible force that left him panting and his heart racing. In addition, he sensed that he was engulfed in fluids. In terror, he reached down to see if he had wet the bed. No, there was nothing on the bed sheets, but he could feel moisture on his stomach under his pajamas. Could something be wrong with him? Was he bleeding or has his body somehow failed? He couldn't turn on a light to see if he was bleeding because it would wake up his sister. The puzzlement stayed with him until morning when, at the first light, he could see nothing on his hand that would indicate anything was amiss. Perhaps he had dreamed the whole thing and it never really happened, but he was unsure.

In his embarrassment that something may be wrong with his man-plumbing, he was reticent to speak to his mother or sister. It was well after breakfast before he could get his father aside to ask if he needed medical attention. After explaining what had happened, Daniel's father suggested that he not worry about his nocturnal emission, that it was completely natural after a boy reaches puberty. He did suggest that Daniel read Genesis 38:8-10 about how a man's 'seed' is the property of God and should not be abused. Onan had wasted his seed and God viewed that as evil and slew him. While Daniel was a bit confounded, he figured that it was just a part of growing up and he wasn't in impending danger, except from God!

That was quite a few years ago and the wasted seed had occurred several other times as he was growing into manhood. Tonight, however was a different story. After Tess and family left, Daniel had a long conversation with Mr. Truesdale. They hit on a wide range of topics regarding business, his newly adopted town, his great aunt and, most comprehensively, Tess.

Evening turned into night and Daniel turned in. Sometime during his sleeping, he started dreaming of this beautiful and desirable young woman. He had never been in love before and was not sure what is real love. Certainly, he had appreciation for all manner of things but, did he *love* them? He thought he loved his parents and sister, however, was that considered love or some other emotion? He thought he loved the mountains of the great Northwest but was it just admiration for the beauty of nature? Surely, he had a wide range of emotions regarding Tess but was she a friend, something beautiful to look at like his mountains or something else? He had only seen her a few times so how, he rationalized, could he think of love. Then there is the physical aspect of love. He had never had sexual relations with a woman but there was something about Tess that stirred up complicated intentions.

The combination of all these feelings drove his dream into areas in which he had never crossed. He certainly knew about sex but had no knowledge of the strength and urgency that physical passion conveyed. In his dream, they were embracing, and she began to touch him. Soon their clothing began to evaporate. As the passion reached a climax, so did young Daniel. The action brought him to awaken just as had earlier wet dreams but his time it was different. It was as if he had actually experienced sexual intercourse with a lover, complete with all the attendant hormonal reactions. Instead of the terror he had experienced as a youth, his whole body now had a glow of wellbeing and the confidence that he was attractive to someone special. In his mind this was an assurance that he was, indeed, falling in love.

The glow did not disappear until after breakfast when his thoughts turned to his great aunt. This was certainly a surprise to learn of an unknown relative in Trail. He dressed in his best and borrowed a tie from Mrs. Truesdale. Mr. Truesdale was still asleep as he had tipped a bit too deeply into the bourbon barrel. She didn't think he would mind. Mrs. Truesdale provided the address and the directions to Aunt Elizabeth's home. They had arranged to have Tess join them after their tea-talk on the way to church.

Upon arrival at Elizabeth's residence, a maid answered the bell and asked Daniel into the foyer and to take a seat. She explained Elizabeth would join him shortly and how did he take his tea? As he waited, he looked around at the paintings and formal furniture. While the rugs were beautiful and furnishings grand, the house had a closed-in old aroma. It was as if the house had been frozen in time sometime near when Daniel was born. The floors would creak, and the rugs were threadbare. However, there was something about the house that had a 'welcoming' appeal. The large windows let in a lot of light through the old wavy glass panes.

Aunt Elizabeth came down the curved staircase dressed in clothing that looked as if they were sewn in the same era that the house was furnished. She was an attractive older woman with shocking silver hair which she wore longer than most of her age's counterparts. She wore what she called 'specks' and gold earrings and neckless. She was small with something of an elfish continence and a warm smile. She was devoid of eyebrows but had cleverly used an eyebrow pencil to mark out the territory where her brows should have been. When she saw Daniel, her smile brightened and the fake brows arched upward.

"Let me look at you Mr. Daniel," she exclaimed as she landed on the foyer. She smiled and remarked how much he favored his father and asked how the family was doing.

"I left Kaak just a couple of weeks ago and so much has happened to me. I was on my way to Vancouver to learn of the ways in the big city but stopped here to earn some cash. My family is doing well, and I am so sorry that they have lost contact with you. I was shocked to learn that I had a relative so close to Kaak. I never really knew my grandparents so that part of my life has always been a mystery."

"Well, Mr. Daniel try one of these scones that Beatrice baked, and I can try to fill you in with some of the details. Your grandmother and I were close in age and in many ways a bit like twins. I was born in 1899 and she arrived in the following year. We were inseparable growing up and spent many years together in the first part of the new century. Just as the new century saw world-wide conflict in 1914, we too were undergoing the struggles of our transformations into young ladies. Girls of that age have trouble coping with their own hormonal issues much less the competition and divergences that invariably come with maturity. We grew apart and went different ways. She eventually married your grandfather who had been a sailor in the Great War and, while I never married, I was a pretty darn sharp businesswoman. By then, we had reconciled our youthful differences and I was asked to attend the christening of your father."

"I guess that was the last time I saw your father. My sister passed not long after his birth and your grandfather moved away, taking the baby with him. He never remarried and was a gruff parent that possibly blamed your father for his wife's death. Last I heard, he had moved down to the States and had taken to heavy drinking but seemed to have an unlimited amount of funds. Your father had a tough childhood but had sent me letters from time to time. He knew how to cope and eventually left home and settled in Kaak, married and started his own family.

"You may not know this, but your birth was difficult on your mother. Sarah was an easy delivery, but you created all kinds of problems. Your father took her to the hospital in Kalispell and it took every bit of money he had just to get her there and into a room. Fortunately, you and your mother survived but the cost was a problem. Your father went to see your grandfather and asked to borrow an amount to cover the hospital stay. I don't know for sure, but something happened between the two and their relationship was severed."

"I wish I knew more. There was talk that your grandfather had found a vein of gold somewhere and he was quietly hoarding a fortune in bullion. He never really settled down but would come through Trail every so often and he invariably came to visit. Perhaps I reminded him of his lost wife and, despite all his faults, he was always a gentleman to me. I think he may have passed away not too long ago but prior to his death, he sent me a peculiar letter. I will look for the letter next week, but my memory is so poor now I hope I can find it somewhere in this monster house."

"Aunt Elizabeth, you mentioned you were a good businessperson. What did you do to afford this grand home?" Asked Daniel.

"Oh, I was able to purchase a little bit of real estate and sold off the timber rights. When the depression hit, I used the income from timber to buy more real estate here in the hills surrounding Trail. As you may know, there has been some findings of trace gold in those very hills. I sometimes sell off mining claims to forty-niners who are willing to pay for the privilege of panning or mining. Of course, I keep the rights for 40% of any findings. I must say I have done fairly well!"

Just then there was a knock at the door and Tess was escorted into the parlor. At her arrival Daniel rose and warmly grasped her hand. Together, they smiled at one another and with mutual visual contact.

Elizabeth stood and begged Tess to join them. Tess exclaimed, "It is so nice to meet you. What a beautiful home."

"We must leave for church in just a few minutes, but please sit and enjoy a scone with us." Elizabeth responded. "Yes, I love this old home and we shall take a tour if you will allow me to offer you both lunches following services?"

"That would be great," blurted Daniel, thinking that this would give him more time with Tess.

Tess said, "I would be delighted. I am going to start college in the fall and I hope to major in design. This house is a wonderful inspiration for me as I begin my studies."

"It's a date then, let me ask Beatrice to add a couple of plates for lunch and we need to head off to church. It's just down the street and we can be there in a couple of minutes."

They walked toward the steeple of the St. Andrew's Anglican Church. As they entered the church, the main body of the congregation recognized, waved or spoke to Elizabeth. Surely, she was an esteemed member and was clearly delighted to be in the company of two attractive young visitors. Heads were turned and whispers ignited as Elizabeth escorted the couple to her normal seat near the alter.

After they sat, the grand organ began to announce the commencement of services. Aunt Elizabeth whispered to Tess and Daniel that the organ was a gift of the Tadanaac Women's Guild as a memorial tribute to Trail's sons that lost their lives during World War II. She told them, "Your friend Mr. Truesdale's son was the impetus of the Guild's decision for the donation. He was heartbroken with his loss and the Guild hoped this gesture could mute some of his grief."

Daniel vowed to himself that, should he ever be in a financial position to make a meaningful contribution to society, he would build a church or school in Kaak.

After services, Aunt Elizabeth suggested that they return to her home for lunch. On the approach to her house, Daniel noted a small cottage in the back yard. Daniel asked, "Is that where Beatrice lives, Aunt Elizabeth?".

"No," she replied, "That is where your grandfather would hang out, whenever he came to visit. It was probably a maid's quarters before I purchased this place. I've only been in it a couple of times, though, Beatrice makes sure it is in top shape."

Tess added, "Can we take a look, seems it has a fireplace and everything?"

"Certainly, my dear, but first let's dine and then I will give you a tour of the whole property, including the cottage."

Lunch was filled with great food and Daniel was happy for his schooling in proper etiquette and endeavored to match the silverware with the meal selection. During lunch he traded glances with Tess and began to feel more comfortable in her presence. Perhaps it was intuition on her part, but she steered the discussions into subjects where he would have commentary. She did not talk about her travels or big-city nuances. Instead, she asked about today's sermon and was surprised when Daniel mentioned that during prayer, he forgave her for the prior day's soap skirmish. For that he received a smile and a pinch on the arm!

Following lunch Elizabeth took the couple room by room and commented on each space as if it was an old friend. Clearly, she had great affection for the old house and attached to all its belongings. Of particular interest to Daniel was her office. Whereas most of the rooms were filled with paintings and mementos of her past, the office where Aunt Elizabeth ran her business was as modern as any major corporation. She had an array of communication equipment, multiple filing cabinets, an adding machine much like at the bank and a large device that Elizabeth indicated was a Xerox copier machine that has just gone on sale in 1959. She had a few photographs of her and various local individuals, one of which she announced was Daniel's grandfather. Daniel looked closely at the picture and noted the resemblance between his father and his grandfather. Tess, too, commented on how Daniel favored them both.

As Daniel looked at his direct lineage, he wondered what happened to break apart such a small family. There was something about the expression of his grandfather in the picture that told of adventures past, of places Daniel had never seen and dangers that had been faced. The expression was of a put-on smile that belied a burden of profound sadness. Truly, his grandfather had a past and had the physical and emotional scars to prove it. He had never even seen a picture of his grandmother but wondered how she must have contributed to the rather sad countenance that peered out from the family photograph. Never would he know of those adventures that led to the man that was his grandfather. Or so he thought!

Elizabeth told them, "While he was not a blood relative to me, he treated me well and, except for his drinking, he was a fine man. To others, he was a scoundrel, perhaps a sentiment that was shared by your father. He was also a shrewd man with his money. I am surprised that he didn't leave anything to his only family. Perhaps he died intestate, he was always so secretive about the source and disposition of his income."

Daniel asked, "What does 'intestate' mean?"

Elizabeth explained that some people never get around to creating a will so when they die the money either goes to the government or is never accounted for. My guess is that he had hidden money in various banks and elsewhere and their location died when he passed away."

Tess expressed an interest in seeing the cottage in the backyard, so Elizabeth led them out the back door along the pathway to the little bungalow. The yard between the house and the cottage was well kept with cut grass and hedges that provided some privacy. Flowers adorned several small gardens that added brightness to the yard. The door was unlocked so they ventured in and both Tess and Daniel were surprised at how open and airy the little two room structure was. The living room was a combination of kitchen and dining room and the bedroom had two windows that let in a lot of the sunlight. As Tess had noted, there was a big fireplace in the living room that projected a cozy feeling to the little house.

Elizabeth noted how complimentary Daniel was regarding the cottage. As they made their way back to the parlor in her home, she remarked, "Daniel, I know you are staying with the Truesdales, but now that I think of it, it may not be too smart to live under the same roof as your boss! They are a wonderful family and I know they ache for the company of a man that may remind them of their son, but some separation would be a smart thing. And, I think that my cottage would make the perfect alternative! It would be good for me too, as you can do some needed chores around here in lieu of rent. It is standing empty now that your grandfather is gone and I hate to see it not being used."

Daniel was at a loss as to how to respond to such sincere kindness, he was so overwhelmed with all the events of the day and the changes in his life. "Aunt Elizabeth, that is such a kind offer. I don't know what to say. May I sleep on it and confer with the Truesdale's before we make any firm decisions? It is too generous an offer!"

"Well, now I am not used to taking no for an answer, but I think when you consider it, you will take me up on the offer! Your grandmother would be so pleased if she is looking down from Heaven. And maybe your grandfather too, but perhaps from a different directional viewpoint."

Tess could tell that Elizabeth was beginning to tire and suggested that she and Daniel head to their respective homes. While Elizabeth feigned vigor, she relented and bid them farewell until tomorrow when she would come calling at the bank to see about his moving to the cottage.

Dream 4, Bit of a Nightmare

While Daniel was dazzled by thoughts of Tess, Sargent Bigsby was reeling from the disrespect he had received from his luncheon with her the prior week. His resentment was starting to consume him, and he blamed the young foreigner for interfering with his romantic pursuits. Rightfully, he was a Mountie, an important pillar of the community, and fancied himself dashing and handsome and the answer to every single woman's desires. He had witnessed Daniel and Tess walking together and wondered how young Tess could prefer a hayseed like Daniel over such a prize as himself.

"Surely," he said to himself, "If I can get that yokel out of town, Tess would invariably fall for me."

It then dawned on the snubbed Sargent that if he could somehow alter Daniel's citizenship paperwork, Daniel would have no choice but to return to Montana. He knew that Superintendent Felps had just received a letter postmarked from Mountie headquarters that was likely the forms Daniel would need to fill out. In his revenge-filled mind, Bigsby decided that he would take the papers and improperly file them. He figured that if he made certain answers sufficiently egregious, the citizenship application would be denied.

That evening, after Felps had left the office, Bigsby took the letter home to complete and then post in the morning. After filling out many of the requests of the document, in the line where it was asked what line of occupation you wish to pursue, Bigsby wrote in 'I hope to engage in extensive beaver trapping and the marketing of their hides'. As an emblem of Canada, the beaver was held in high regard and, due to unregulated trapping, was nearly extinct in the mid-19th century. To have a foreign-born person seeking citizenship by trapping a national symbol would certainly raise eyebrows at headquarters. Bigsby forged Daniel's signature and sent the reply off to Mountie headquarters the next morning.

Meanwhile, Daniel had returned to the Truesdale's home and discussed Aunt Elizabeth's proposal regarding the cottage. While both Mr. and Mrs. Truesdale agreed that the offer was attractive, Daniel could sense that they both wished he would stay. Aunt Elizabeth's words, "It may not be too smart to live under the same roof as your boss," echoed in his brain and seemed wise advice. Daniel expressed how fond he was of them both and how grateful he was that they had opened their home to him but was steadfast that he should leave. They consented, as he explained how young men need their privacy, particularly if they are falling in love.

That comment sealed the deal with Mrs. Truesdale, "We certainly don't want to stand in the way of romance! Like I said before, 'this ole town needs some fresh feelings and something for the townsfolk to whisper about'! You must come back though, every week for dinner just to keep us up to date with how things are going with you and Lady Tess! I want to be the first to know exactly what is happening with this burgeoning romance before those girls at the card parties!"

While that night Sargent Bigsby dreamed of revenge, Daniel's bedtime adventures started with a sweet dream of Tess. In the morning Bigsby awoke with a bitter taste in his mouth and the weariness that comes from a fitful half-sleep. Daniel's slumber was pretty much the same. What started out as a warm and romantic dream about Tess, the further into his dream, the more apprehension he sensed. In his dream the couple were having a picnic beside the Columbia River that ran through Trail. It was a beautiful day and she was radiant in a bright blue dress that mirrored the summer sky. Suddenly, the waters of that mighty river started to boil and a flash flood from up in the mountains made it way downstream. They tried to run toward higher ground but the waters were rising too rapidly. He woke with a start just as Tess was being ripped from his grasp by the floodwaters. His heart was racing and he was wet with sweat as he climbed out of bed to rinse off his face. He was trembling a bit when he arose but was relieved that this experience was all in his mind and not reality. Nevertheless, country people believe in omens and this was certainly something that would stay in Daniel's mind and psyche.

Daniel went downstairs for his last breakfast with the Truesdales. As he had become accustomed to their camaraderie in the mornings, this was a bitter-sweet meal that left all three with a tear. They hugged one another following breakfast. Daniel said his goodbye to Mrs. Truesdale and he and Mr. Truesdale headed off to the office. Work was becoming fun for Daniel and he still got to see Mr. Truesdale several times during the morning. Sure enough, at ten o'clock sharp, in waltzed Aunt Elizabeth to press her offer regarding the cottage. Daniel greeted her with a sincere hug and explained that he had discussed the proposal with the Truesdales and he would be delighted to move into the cottage. Elizabeth beamed and said that he should pack his bag and come over that evening to tidy up the place and put his personal stamp on his new lodging.

About that time Gus and Tess showed up at the bank. "So, it seems that you and your great aunt have become acquainted." Gus exclaimed as he joined the two.

Before Daniel could respond, Elizabeth exclaimed, "Why yes, indeed Gus, and I surely am fond of him and your beautiful daughter! They cut quite a figure in the town and to these old eyes of mine."

"I agree, they make a handsome couple," issued Gus making both Tess and Daniel blush at their portrayal as a 'couple'.

Elizabeth then remarked to Gus, "Can I borrow you for a couple of minutes in private, Gus? I have something to ask you about Daniel's grandfather."

As Elizabeth pulled Gus aside, Tess expressed her embarrassment at her father's remark about their status to Daniel.

"Not to worry, I sort of liked what he said." To which Tess gave a big smile and a wink!

"Well, I had better get back on the teller line, looks like business is picking up."

With that Daniel said his good-byes to Tess and Gus and returned to work. Not long after that, Sargent Bigsby strolled in and Daniel asked if he could help him.

"No," replied Bigsby, "I want to deal with a real teller. And, by the way, tell my girlfriend Tess that I said 'hello'."

Daniel knew Bigsby was trying to push his buttons, so he decided not to fall into that trap. "Will be more than happy to and, I think there is a 'real' teller at the next lane."

Bigsby conducted his business while constantly glaring at Daniel the entire time. All the while, Daniel smiled and maintained his cheerful demeanor, which aggravated the Mountie even more. Bigsby thought, as soon as he gets rejected on his citizenship, we will see that smile wiped off his cornpone face.

The dramatic episode between the two did not escape the watchful eye of Mr. Truesdale. After Bigsby left, Truesdale subtlety asked Daniel to join him in his office.

"I saw the way you handled the Mountie just now. You were very smart not to irritate him. And, from the looks he gave you, your method of dealing with the situation probably infuriated him even more than if you had been antagonistic. You have a level of maturity that far exceeds your twenty some years."

"Thank you, sir, I wouldn't want to do anything that might reflect badly on you or the bank. He seems to have some ire with me though I have done nothing to him nor even have had a conversation. I'm pretty sure he has a 'thing' for Tess and I am in the way. I know he is the law but he better not push me too far or do anything to harm Tess or her reputation."

"I think that we need to rotate your training toward the lending side of the bank. That is where we make money and a good lending officer has many of the qualities that you have shown me in the little time we have known one another. I have a book on banking processes that I would like you to read….that is if you have any spare time ALONE."

That last little inuendo was clearly a reference to how the two lovebirds seemed to be spending a lot of time together.

After work that day Daniel met Tess at the diner and they sat down for a quick meal. In walked Bigsby who turned around and went back outside after seeing the two together. Neither of the couple saw Bigsby so they continued to have a pleasant dinner and then strolled over to Elizabeth's house. There she greeted them and led them to the cottage. She gave Daniel a key and showed him how to work the fireplace flue, how to prime the water faucet and where cleaning chemicals were kept. She moved with great pace, as she was well aware of being the third wheel and was sure the couple would enjoy a few moments alone. Elizabeth said her good-byes and expressed her happiness that her great nephew had moved into her cottage. She was right about the need for the couple to be alone as, almost immediately after she shut the door, Tess came up to Daniel and kissed him fully on the lips.

At that particular moment, Daniel knew his life had changed forever. He returned her kiss and wrapped his arm around her shoulders. Maybe he was starting to know what love really is all about and how different it is from his earlier thoughts. Yes, he treasured her friendship, and yes, he marveled at her beauty, but he had never considered the fact that she was surrendering part of her soul to him. As was he to her. Instead of surrender being a weakness, it was the strength of two souls bound together. Two spirits that found a common desire, a common need and a common bond.

As Daniel walked Tess home, there was a marked degree of restraint in their conversation. Both were deep in thoughts about what had just happened and what the future held. They were surely in love and first love is eternally filled with the most powerful emotions and, at the same time, is the most confounding. For each, there was no point of reference, no history from which to draw. It was as if the climb from adolescence to adulthood happened in that very instant. As sweet as were their love thoughts, both felt some anxiety over what would happen when Tess went off to college in a few months. Consequently, wrapped in their thoughts, neither happened to notice the shadowy figure of Sargent Bigsby following along behind.

Bigsby had been watching through the window of the cottage that was now Daniel's new home. He saw their embrace which served only to steady his resolve in getting Daniel out of town, out of the country. The glow which shone on Tess's face fueled Bigsby's desire to have this lovely young beauty. He wanted that same response when he would be kissing her. As he followed them to Tess's house, he envisioned significantly embarrassing Daniel in front of Tess and Mr. Truesdale. Certainly, when the citizenship rejection came in, he could march Daniel out of the bank in hand cuffs and out of his life forever. Maybe he would even receive a commendation for ridding the community of a notorious trapper from the States. He was smiling to himself as Tess and Daniel bid a good night with a brief kiss. He would have his revenge and he would have the girl.

The following morning, Daniel woke to Aunt Elizabeth's knock at the door. She asked him if the accommodations were acceptable and would he join her for breakfast. "I had a wonderful sleep and would love to have breakfast."

Elizabeth responded, "Well, I am glad you like the place. It needed some 'life' after your grandfather passed, God rest his soul. I will have Beatrice add a plate. She makes the absolute best omelets! Do you like cheese?”

“I certainly do and will be right over after I take a quick shower. I need to get to the bank and may have overslept a bit.”

At breakfast, Aunt Elizabeth explained that she had found the letter that his grandfather had posted for her prior to his death. Again, she reiterated that the letter was confusing, and she didn’t understand a lot of what he was trying to explain to her. It was almost written to be unintelligible, as if some parts were in a code that she didn’t understand. There were mathematical expressions mixed in with commentary that simply made no obvious connection. She suggested that Daniel look at the letter and see if he could make out what his grandfather was trying to convey. While Daniel was interested in solving the riddle of the letter, he explained that he needed to get to the bank. “Perhaps we can look at the letter together tonight when I get home. Maybe I can use that as an excuse to have Tess drop by as well!”

“Oh, I don’t think you need an excuse to have her come over. She seems willing enough!” noted the wily Elizabeth.

That morning at the bank Mr. Truesdale introduced Daniel to each of the lending officers and indicated that he would be rotating through their division to gain some knowledge of what the lending function was all about. They had noticed Daniel in the teller line and taken note that he was becoming a favorite of Truesdale. As in all corporate settings, newcomers were viewed somewhat as a threat. Mr. Truesdale understood he was throwing Daniel into the lion's den. He figured that Daniel would either make friends or he would learn by experiencing the realities of corporate competition. Daniel was given a chair but no desk. He would move his chair around to the desks of the lenders as they each had clients come in. In the periods while there were no clients, the lenders would explain the various aspects of how loans were processed, how to assess risk and the role of interest rates in providing the profits to the bank. He also was told of the darker side of lending which is the default on a loan. Daniel had heard of ranchers who had lost their property when they couldn't repay the bank. It was always viewed as an evil thing that banks do to their customers. He was starting to learn the other side of the equation. Just as the ranch was an asset of the rancher, so was the collateral of the loan, an asset to the bank. There was nothing sinister or evil intent by the bank. They would not wish to have a loan go into default because of the time, effort and cost of dealing with collateral liquidation.

Daniel asked a lot of questions, just as he had on the teller line. His natural honesty and friendly nature helped him with the loan officers. In turn, the officers helped him to understand the jargon of the banking industry. Portfolios, legal lending limits, prime rate, credit scores, loan docs., collateral, default, terms, amortization and a myriad of other foreign sounding names were thrust upon him. One of the officers good naturedly played a trick on Daniel when he told him that he was about to LIBOR a customer that had a serious accretion on his balance sheet. When Daniel just nodded his head, the lenders each got a good laugh. Daniel took the ribbing in his easy-going fashion and laughed a little at himself. That humility helped him overcome the loan officers' natural need to protect their 'turf'.

Aunt Elizabeth had called Tess that afternoon to ask if she would like to come over for dinner. Tess had to decline as she was preparing dinner for the family. After Elizabeth explained about the letter, Tess asked if they could get together after dinner to see about unraveling the mysterious last letter. Tess could hardly contain her excitement about seeing Daniel and the challenge that might be presented by the enigmatic dispatch.

That evening Daniel dined with his great aunt and they discussed their respective day's activities. Daniel was surprised to hear that Elizabeth had taken her jeep up to the smelter and hiked around the mountainside. The smelter was a major employer in

Trail and offered her a safe place to park the car and easy access to the many trails in the surrounding mountains. Daniel expressed his concern about her age and the dangers that can befall anyone in the remote wilderness.

"I can certainly take care of myself and have lived loving these mountains all my life. To keep me away would be cruel and, besides, I carry my pistol, a compass and a flash light just in case. Always be prepared is my motto and it has served me well for decades. Now, I admit that I can't go as far on my hikes as I once could, but I figure a half hour in and half out back out is fine given the shape I'm in. So, don't you go fretting about me, I am just fine. The mountains have always replaced the fact that I never married. The trees and cliffs are my husband and the sounds and smells of the hills are my lovers."

In turn, Daniel explained how he had been working with the lending officers and some of what he had learned.

"I'm glad that Mr. Truesdale had you go through that rotation. If you ever want to make banking your career, whether you stay here or move to Vancouver, you are best served by a good understanding of how to make loans."

Daniel had completely forgotten about his expedition to the 'big city'. "Oh, Aunt Elizabeth, I think Trail suits me just fine right now. I have never met so many nice people and there is one in particular that I really want to spend more time getting to know."

"Well, she should be here any minute now and maybe the three of us can unlock the mysteries of your grandfather's letter. While he was a strange bird, when he was sober he was sharp as a tack and extremely intuitive. There were always a lot of rumors flying around about him but no one seems to fully understand much about his life and his fortune. He was certainly not lacking for funds as he always traveled first class, always dressed well, ate well and was passionate for his Crown Royal whisky."

The doorbell rang and Daniel jumped up to answer the calling. In walked Tess and Daniel could feel his heart beating in his temples. It was all he could do to restrain himself from kissing her right in front of Aunt Elizabeth.

"Well, hello Miss Tess, thank you for coming over this evening. Maybe we can figure out what Daniel's grandfather was trying to express. I hope he wrote it when sober but I wouldn't be surprised if he was dead drunk. I have it here so let's lay it out on the table and have a look and see if we can make heads or tails of what the ole guy was trying to convey."

Aunt Elizabeth was certainly correct when she said it was unusual. The writing was shaky and difficult to read, and you could tell it was not completed all at once. There were symbols and the dialogue was not that of a normal course of communication. The whole composition was handwritten in script on two pages of standard typewriter paper. At the bottom there were numbers, separated by commas, that were in black and red, with the red numbers underlined. The text read:

My Dearest Elizabeth,

I hope this letter finds its way to you. I don't have confidence in POSTs where I am. Certain bad people have been watching me with evil intent. I have not been doing too well of late. I would give my fame and fortune to feel better. My heart rate is only 49 and the degree of my liver function is .057. The doctor says my blood pressure is 117 over 90 and since I turned 72, my age is against me. The biggest issue, however, is of an old bachelor bladder problem. I only have a small stream any more.

I hope you are WELL and your direction in life remains steadfast. Your heart is as good as gold. If you need to reach me try me at:

41,62,205,16,443,10056,88,15030,609,107,1102,1101,
51,1004,12023,208110,129,629,62,604,8010,9821.

'Well," stated Elizabeth, "Your grandfather was definitely worried about this particular letter falling into the wrong hands. He made many enemies in his life and many coveted his financial resources. I can only presume that he was trying to warn us or hint to us something about his life. The reference to his bladder problem is so crass that I cannot believe he would mention it to me unless it is some form of code."

"Aunt Elizabeth, certainly the numbers at the bottom are too many to be any type of telephone number or post box. Perhaps this is the code that he used just in case of the letter was intercepted." Spoke Tess. "The numbers are in no particular sequence and range from double digits to six digits."

Daniel chimed in, "Perhaps if we take just the black numbers and apply them to the corresponding letter itself, that may give us the clue."

When they tried taking the 4th and 6th and 20th and 16th and 44th and 100th of the initial numbers and corresponded them to the sequence of the words, the sentence read: 'letter its bad where fortune more'.

"Well, that doesn't make any sense, let's try just using the red number and try the same way."

The 1st, 2nd 5th, 3rd and 56th words ended up with: 'I hope finds this degree'.

"That's not any more coherent than using just the black numbers."

They mulled over the content of the letter, looked to see if there was any hidden messages or other clues as to the nature and intent of the passage. After an hour or so they agreed to give up. While a bit disappointed in their inability to cipher the letter, Daniel was excited to walk Tess home that evening. They held hands and walked the slow walk of two that really didn't want to reach their destination in any hurry. At her doorstep they embraced and Tess touched his lips with her tongue. Daniel had heard of French kissing but that touch created a tingle that went all the way to his toes. He opened his mouth a little and allowed his tongue to explore her mouth. By now he was sweating and things started happening below his belt. At about that time the porch light came on and Gus walked out the front door. Immediately, the couple disengaged. Daniel muttered a weak, "Hello, Gus how are you this evening."

Gus replied, "Just getting ready for my evening stroll. Gotta keep active and, for a big guy like me, I just can't get any exercise during the heat of the day."

Daniel thought but didn't say, "Yes, I was starting to get big myself!"

With that, the couple said their goodbyes and Daniel walked back to the cottage, his head filled with exhilaration over the kiss and the letter.

When he arrived home, he decided to explore the little cottage. The day's events had filled him with energy and he didn't feel like sleeping. He wanted to get a better familiarity with his new residence, take a good look at the pictures, clean up the shower, dust the bookcase and maybe test out the stovetop by making a cup of tea. As he worked his way around the rooms, the sounds of his boots on the floor seemed to vary. In one particular spot beside the fireplace, there appeared to be something of a hollow sound and didn't provide as steady a feel. He closely inspected the site and happened to notice an adjacent lever on the side of the hearth. It was obscure but Daniel thought it might be a release for ashes. As he pulled up on the lever, a small space of the wood floor slid into a slot on the side of the hearth. What remained was a two foot by two-foot hole in the floor. Anxiously, Daniel sought a flashlight to peer down into the abyss. Under the sink, he recalled that Elizabeth had stored various tools and, indeed, there was a flashlight.

He shown the beam into the hole and immediately noticed there was a crude ladder that led below. Daniel tested the rungs and they seemed secure, so he stepped down into this hidden basement. When he reached the dirt floor, he found himself in a tunnel that led away from the cottage. He followed the narrow passage for at least a hundred feet before the trail ended in another ladder upward. As he climbed upward, he thought that this must have been dug by his grandfather to possibly avoid his enemies. He had seen other such escape tunnels in old cabins that frontiersmen had dug to get away from Indian raids. When he reached the top rung there was a wooden handle carved into a circular piece of timber. Daniel had to use all his considerable might to push up the handle and clear the exit. Indeed, the hole was filled expertly by an old stump that was invisibly hinged to tilt over. As he climbed out, he found himself in a vacant lot that was overgrown with weeds and bushes. He and Tess had passed that area several times on the way to her house but had never paid any attention. Daniel climbed back down the ladder, pulling the stump back atop the exit hole and returned to the cottage. There he shifted back the fireplace lever and the flooring returned to cover the tunnel entrance. He sat for a moment contemplating the effort that it must have taken to construct the escape passage and why the tunnel was necessary. Surely, his grandfather must have been very cautious about how and when he used Aunt Elizabeth's little guesthouse.

The next morning, Daniel headed off to work, his head filled with excitement and dizzying thoughts.

His grandfather's letter, the intrigue associated with the hidden tunnel, the relationship he was building with his great aunt, his love with Tess and the education he was receiving at the bank occupied his attention. Little did he know what was about to befall that could put all that asunder.

The morning began as usual, he spoke to Mr. Truesdale and the ladies at the teller line, he sat with one of the lending officers and would occasionally read a passage in the book that Truesdale had provide him. At about eleven, in walked Tess and her family to see Mr. Truesdale. Gus had decided to make some real estate purchases in the community and wanted advice on mortgages. Mr. Truesdale ushered Gus into his office and Tess came by where Daniel was working. As they chatted all the other loan officer took note and smiled to each other regarding their new comrade.

Meanwhile, Sargent Bigsby had convinced Superintendent Felps that they had a duty to rid the community of the alien whose citizenship had been denied in the morning post. In fact, since there hadn't been much activity in the town of late, why not show the citizens that they were on top of the legal process and make a public demonstration of the arrest? While Felps was generally a decent guy and would have normally perform his job quietly and with discretion, he was led astray by Bigsby's grandiose plan. Nonetheless, he acquiesced and accompanied Bigsby to the bank to handcuff and arrest Daniel as an illegal alien.

As the Mounties marched into the bank all eyes were upon them. It was as if a bank robbery was in progress and they were there to save the day. Instead, they paraded up to Daniel and, much to his astonishment, placed him in handcuffs. With Tess cries, both Gus and Mr. Truesdale emerged from the office.

Mr. Truesdale shouted, "What is going on here?"

Bigsby stated, "We are arresting this illegal immigrant as he is duly working in a financial institution and has not received an approval for citizenship. That is a breach of law and he will be deported after fines and processing." There was a collective gasp by employees and customers alike and Tess was in tears.

To which Mr. Truesdale responded in his calm and confident manner, "I am sorry, but you are both mistaken. Daniel received his citizenship papers last week when he and I met with Circuit Judge Nelson. You may not know, but Daniel's mother is not only Canadian but also of the tribal nation. Nelson was happy to issue the documents for Daniel's rightful Canadian citizenry. His passport is on the way and his great aunt and I are going to work to get him a driver's license! Now I suggest you unfetter the young lad and apologize to him and all present. I have never witnessed such insolence by Trail's law enforcement!"

The totally embarrassed Superintendent Felps was beside himself with apologies and contrite on the matter. Bigsby, on the other hand, was irate and completely humiliated by his failures in front of his boss, in front of Tess, and in front of some of the city's most influential citizens. His failure poured even more salt into the wounds he had already experienced with Daniel and Tess. He knew he would get a tongue lashing from Felps and this misadventure could possibly cost him his job. After a half-hearted apology, he quickly escaped to the street and started the walk back to the stationhouse. Felps caught up with him and did, as expected, blast Bigsby's attitude and ineptness in handling the whole affair. He suggested that Bigsby should write an apology to Daniel and Mr. Truesdale or he could seek alternative employment. Bigsby growled a response that he would but the bile arose from his throat and the venom for Daniel was only heightened. He blamed Daniel for all his woes, and he would continue to extract his revenge. Maybe not now, but certainly in the future and he would relish the day when he could best the young foreigner.

As Mr. Truesdale was apologizing to the staff and to the customers that happened to be in the bank during the Mountie interruption, everyone was beginning to go back to normalcy. Even Daniel, who was certainly embarrassed and enraged over the episode had regained his composure and had resumed working with the lending officers. A calm prevailed over the bank lobby and all were going about their normal business. All except for Gus! For several reasons Gus had become very fond of young Daniel and figured there was more to the story than a simple mistaken communication. He followed the Mounties back to their headquarters and went around to the back door of their office and listened to the conversation through an open window. He listened as Sargent Bigsby tried to explain how regional headquarters had gotten so confused with Daniel's citizenship. Felps was having none of Bigsby's explanation and finally got a confession that Bigsby had, indeed, altered the fraudulent paperwork.

"Why in the name of God would you do such a stupid thing?" Felps interrupted Bigsby's dialogue. "You are sworn to uphold the law, not break regulations. And for what reason? Has the kid done anything to you? You have had an exemplary service record until now and this thing makes no sense to me!"

Bigsby countered, "There are rumors that Daniel's grandfather is that notorious gangster that used to hang around here. I can't recall his name but he was the brother-in-law that churchwoman Elizabeth. I just felt Daniel was a potential danger to the community. No one knew how his grandfather got all his money, but some thought he was involved in a spectacular bank robbery in Vancouver a few years back. Since Daniel is working at a bank and seems to have 'snowed' the bank's owner, I figured 'the acorn doesn't fall far from the tree'. Hell, we don't know if the grandfather is still alive and using his grandson to case the bank for a potential heist."

"Ok, now that makes some sense" noted Felps. " We will keep a close eye on our newest Canadian, but this doesn't let you off the hook just yet. I will have to fill out a report to regional for the record. I will try to avoid suggesting any penalties and regional usually pushes any disciplinary action down to the local office. While I am not happy with you, I think I understand your concerns, which may be actually commendable, if accurate. That is all, Sargent."

As Gus listened to Bigsby's tale he was well aware that Bigsby was lying. He knew how Daniel's grandfather had amassed his fortune and it wasn't from stealing. In fact, he was the subject of several thefts himself of the gold that he had mined. No one knew from where the gold came but it certainly wasn't from a bank!

At Bigsby's dismissal, Gus headed back to the bank. There he had a long chat with Mr. Truesdale in his office then walked over to Daniel's chair along the chain of desks belonging to the loan officers. He asked Daniel to join his family for dinner that evening.

Daniel asked, "Gus, what do you think of this Mountie issue? I hope it hasn't shaken Tess. I promise, I haven't done anything wrong to embarrass her."

"That's not why I want you to come over this evening. Tess is enamored with you and her mother and I find you an admirable suitor. However, we are committed that she attend college in the fall. We want the best for our only child and she has a lot of talent in design and decorating."

Daniel went back to working with one of the loan officers who was involved in the analysis of a company that had applied for a loan. "Daniel, here is a company that was doing well then, all of a sudden, its earnings slipped into the red for two consecutive quarters. What would you make of that? Was there some change in their products, management issues, the general economy or some other external event that altered the course of a good earnings trend?" asked one of the lending staff. After some discussion and evaluation, both Daniel and the officer came to the same conclusion. The company needed a loan to modernize its production facility to compete with imports from Japan. The officer suggested they visit the plant and get a first-hand understanding of how the loan could help resurrect the profit flow.

While all this was being discussed the officer's comment of the company's earnings being 'in the red' returned Daniel's thoughts to his grandfather's letter. Perhaps his grandfather was using the red numbers as part of the code. In business red always refers to the negative. Conceivably, to further obfuscate the letter's code, perhaps the red numbers should be subtracted from the black numbers to create a 'new' number that should be applied to the words. He would have to check that out when he returned to the cottage.

Following work, Daniel hurried home. He had a lot to think about. Certainly, the day was filled with drama from the Mounties. He still did not fully understand why he was being singled out by the legal authorities, but he was pleased that Mr. Truesdale had the foresight to confirm his citizenship. He was pretty sure that Sargent Bigsby hated him due to the Tess situation, but had underestimated how far Bigsby would take the issue. Also, he was looking forward to exploring the hidden tunnel further. In his haste to uncover the tunnel's destination, he did not inspect the corridor as closely as he should and wanted to spend some time poking around. Certainly, he was looking forward to dinner at Gus's house and seeing Tess. Funny it was Gus that offered the invitation and not her. That mattered not - he was going to see Tess tonight and that was all that he cared about. Perhaps she could come over after dinner and help him review the letter to see if his theory regarding the red and black numbers could uncover any message that his grandfather may have intended for Elizabeth. Yes, the evening held many promises!

As soon as he arrived back at the cottage he changed into his jeans and boots. He really wanted to see the tunnel again and grabbed the flashlight and opened the entrance. Climbing down the little wooden ladder he noted that it was particularly well made. The rungs were inlaid into the frame and were quite sturdy. The cavern dropped some nine feet before his feet touched ground. He could see that the tunnel was not in a straight line as it appeared to be excavated around larger rocks that dominated much of the Trail's landscape. As he worked his way down the tunnel he had to hunch down a bit as the height of the shaft was about five feet in height. He calculated that there was probably four feet of soil covering the passageway. Looking at the ceiling, he noticed that there were supporting crossbeams like in a mine to help avoid any potential cave-ins. Daniel found it interesting that somebody, presumably his grandfather, hand dug this tunnel in a manner much like a gold miner might. As he worked his way to the exit ladder, Daniel noticed a Stetson sitting on a nail on the side of the ladder. He hadn't noticed it in his initial journey through the tunnel. This being the only thing in the subway, he returned to the cottage to look at the hat. Replacing the hidden entranceway, Daniel sat down to more fully examine the hat. It was a premium winter Stetson made of pressed beaver felt. It was large, surely bigger than Daniel could wear. On the inside of the brim his grandfather's initials were engraved. He also recalled that photo that Elizabeth had of his grandfather and father. That hat looked exactly like the hat in the photo. Now, Daniel was certain that it was his flesh and blood that had constructed the shaft and had used it to enter and leave the cottage without anyone seeing. Did he have that many enemies that he needed an escape route? There were many mysteries yet to be solved!

As he was reviewing the hat-band he noticed that it was thicker in some sectors than in others. He decided to remove the band and, when he pulled it off the hat some sand fell onto his lap. Or at least he thought it was sand but upon further inspection it looked a lot like gold dust. He carried the band over to the dinner table and laid out the band on a plate. He cut the seam of the band open and to his surprise, he poured out about an ounce of pure gold dust.

Daniel quickly placed the dust into a glass jar and tightly closed the lid. He had no idea of its worth but knew it was important for several reasons. First, it was hidden just like any other cache that man or animal sets aside for emergencies. Secondly, it was suggestive of the potential for other 'finds' that his grandfather had made that may be uncovered in the clues of his letter. Finally, the construction of the tunnel was indicative of someone who had been familiar with mining and not of panning for gold. Mining always represented the potential for a gold vein which could amount to a significant discovery. Panned gold finds, however, were usually streaky and invariably came following heavy rainfall when the creeks were swollen and lighter minerals were washed away. Daniel pondered the ramifications of the tunnel and gold that he had stumbled upon. While he was elated and thrilled with the prospects of his grandfather's gold, he felt he needed to share this information with Elizabeth and Gus. Both knew his grandfather and that knowledge could help him interpret the code of the letter as well as the comings and goings of his grandfather.

Meanwhile, fortified with several happy hour beers, several of the loan officers decided to set up a prank on Daniel based upon the Mounties' fiasco. They knew that the city had an outdoor display on 'all things Canadian' wherein was a mannequin that was dressed like a Mountie. It just took a quick jump over a fence after dark to obtain the full size mannequin complete in military uniform, holstered fake firearm and plastic handcuffs. The loan officers took the Mountie to the back door of the bank and left if for tomorrow when the bank would open. They thought it would be quite funny to have the 'Mountie' awaiting poor Daniel with handcuffs at ready.

Gus had two agendas for the evening's discussion. First, he wanted to inform Daniel and Tess to be cautious around the Mounties. He would relay the overheard conversation and tell of both Bigsby's lies as well as his 'duping' of Felps. They were still the law and it was not out of the question that even legal authorities can bend laws to suit their agenda. He was particularly concerned for Daniel and the background painted by Bigsby of his grandfather's false bank heist. If Bigsby was bold enough to falsify official documents, he certainly could come up with a scheme that could compromise Daniel's banking status. Also, he had a strong idea that Bigsby's hatred of Daniel had more to do with Tess than some unknown boy from Montana. Gus was very protective of his only child and was wary of someone that might be obsessed with her.

Second on his agenda was to have a frank discussion on the nature of the growing relationship between his daughter and Daniel. He well knew of the power of hormones at their ages and he was concerned for both their futures. He had worked hard all his life to ensure that his daughter could get a quality higher education and felt she had a real talent. He liked Daniel but was worried that the two had become so wrapped up in each other that his perception of Tess's future might be altered. He would ask them to be prepared to pursue non-romantic goals. Daniel needed to learn how to become a good lending officer and Tess needed to concentrate on her studies in the fall. Like all parents, however, he was prepared for his conversation and warnings to fall upon deaf ears.

When Daniel arrived, flushed with the exciting news of his two discoveries, Gus's whole dialogue plan changed. An adventurer himself, he was as excited as was Daniel with the discoveries of the hidden chamber and the gold dust. Likewise, Tess was thrilled with the prospect of deciphering the letter and following the mystery of grandfather's gold. Daniel explained everything that had led to the discovery of the hidden tunnel and the finding of the Stetson. He was convinced that he was walking in his grandfather's shoes and finding the answer to so many questions. Most importantly was his theory that the code within his grandfather's letter might be revealed if he correctly assumed the red numbers should be subtracted from the black letters. He brought the letter for the family to review and decipher.

The dinner was dispatched of quickly as everyone was eager to look at the letter and see if they could understand what was concealed. After all the dishes were put away the whole family gathered in the den. At Daniel's urging, Gus had called Elizabeth and asked her to come over. As soon as she arrived and was filled in on the tunnel and the hat, they sat down to look at the letter.

"My goodness, a lot has happened in the last few weeks!" exclaimed Elizabeth. "It's like Trail goes for years with nothing more exciting than the smelter owner's son arrested for having a few pot cigarettes and now we have a hidden tunnel, a proverbial message in a bottle, and mysterious gold dust in an old cap! How intriguing!"

As the group assembled around the dining room table, Daniel laid out the letter and a separate blank paper. There he took the red numbers and subtracted them from the black that were connected within the commas. When he did, the numbers came out to

3,4,15,16,41,44,88,120,51,107,108,109,51,96,97,98,12
9,53,62,56,70,77. Then he circled the corresponding
words. When the group read the circled words, the
message was most definitely a coded instruction for
Aunt Elizabeth. The words of the sentence read,
'This letter posts where my fortune of gold is and
your direction is a small stream at 49 .057 degree
117 72.'

When they had read the passage they were thrilled to
realize that the code had been broken but unsure as
to exactly what the final numbers meant. Clearly,
Daniel's grandfather wanted Elizabeth to know how
to find his treasure that was beside or in a small
stream. But what was the meaning of 49.057 degree
117 72? Daniel's education had not taken him into
geography however, Gus had an immediate
understanding of longitude and latitude lines. As a
world traveler and an international gold trader he
was familiar with the geographic coordinate system
that utilized celestial navigation to pinpoint any place
on earth. Gus explained that early sailors utilized
angular measurements of celestial bodies and the
horizon to determine their precise location. This
must be the clue that Daniel's grandfather meant as
to how to find his 'fortune'. Unfortunately, none of
the group had any way to use the numbers to map
out where this location might be in the world. They
would have to wait until tomorrow when a map
could be reviewed at the library to get an idea of

how to find this part of Grandfather's clue. Daniel had to work in the morning and Tess was going to a design lecture, so it was agreed that Gus and Elizabeth would meet in the morning to seek out the answers that would lead to the letter's intent.

As Elizabeth left and Gus and his wife took the dishes back to the kitchen Daniel and Tess would kiss whenever the dining room was empty. Not the best of 'make-out' opportunities, but the young lovers were desperate to have those special moments. Each time a set of dishes were heading to the kitchen sink, Daniel would pull her to him and feel that electricity whenever their lips met. Daniel was starting to also experience her breasts against his chest as they pressed together. Unfortunately, Gus walked in on them and asked them to sit down for a minute. Hating to throw cold water on the excitement of the evening Gus said, "I know you two are going through a phase of your life that generations since Adam and Eve have experienced. I just want to warn you about wrapping your future based upon what seem like overwhelming and permanent emotions. In the words of the French philosopher, Marcel Proust, 'Alas, it is the human condition that we make our most irrevocable decisions based upon a state of mind that is destined not to last.' Please keep that in mind. Life is long and you will both make many decisions in your time on earth and you might just keep the words of Mr. Proust in the top of your mind."

"Oh, Daddy! You are so sweet, but we understand. Daniel is a wonderful friend and I just couldn't see me liking anyone any better." She hesitated substituting 'liking' for 'loving', which is what her heart and mind were telling her. She didn't want to worry her father anymore and run the risk of having him prohibiting the growing relationship.

"Ok," said her father, knowing that she was playing with him. "Just heed my words."

As he was leaving, he gave Daniel a glance and a raised eyebrow. Daniel understood the awkward moment and smiled shyly. He was head over heels for Tess but didn't want to jeopardize his relationship with Gus. He would simply have to be more in control of his emotions (and desires!).

Tess walked Daniel out to the front porch where she gave him a powerful embrace and extended goodnight kiss. Much to his surprise, her hand slid down from his back to the top of his buttocks in a gesture that indicated either passion or defiance to her father's warnings. Daniel almost gasped at the signal but quickly regained his composure and his hands began to wander in a like fashion. While the embrace lasted only a few seconds, it established a new frontier for the couple. When the kiss ended both were flushed and their hearts were racing. They both said goodnight and their glances underscored the changing relationship. Neither smiled at the departure but their eyes danced at the prospect of the new steps of intimacy that their relationship was developing.

The next morning Daniel walked to work and as he entered the bank, he noticed that the tellers were watching him. As he turned the corner to the loan section of the bank, Mr. Truesdale stepped out of his office to greet Daniel. This seemed strange since Truesdale generally was focused on his sorting of the morning's activities and prioritizing for the day. As he approached, a couple of the loan officers were standing in front of his chair discussing something about the hockey offseason. As Daniel got closer, they parted and, sitting in his chair, was a Mountie with hands extended and handcuffs dangling. Daniel instinctively gasped and stepped back. As the loan and teller staff burst into laughter Daniel realized that the Mountie was a prop and he was the butt of their joke. As he laughed at himself, Mr. Truesdale came up to him and took the handcuffs and told Daniel that he was going to handcuff him to his chair until he learned enough to become a lending officer. The two officers picked up the Mountie and took him back to the display down the street. Truesdale put his arm around Daniel's shoulders and told him he was proud how he was able to laugh at himself and not take the innocent play too seriously. "You probably made a lot of friends today, Daniel." He said. "Winning the hearts of your co-workers is a critical step in becoming a leader! You passed that with flying colors."

Daniel responded, "Mr. Truesdale, there is something that I would like to talk to you about regarding my recent discoveries. Can we go into your office for a few minutes?" Daniel related the events of the past evening regarding the tunnel, the gold dust and the coded letter. He left out the details of the romantic issues, however!

After listening to the story, Truesdale told Daniel two things. First, he should open a lock box and keep the gold dust safe. Secondly, he should take up Elizabeth's offer to teach him how to drive. He said that Elizabeth's old jeep would be a perfect vehicle for him to learn the skill and he suspected she would be happy to loan him the car whenever he needed to go further than he could walk. Daniel agreed and, together they called Elizabeth to see when she could tutor him on the laws and nuances of driving. She heartily agreed to assist him that evening if he had the time. She said that she had to hurry off the call, however, because Gus was at the door and they were heading to the library. She suggested that they both meet at the diner for lunch and talk about what they might uncover at the library regarding the latitude and longitude clue. She mentioned that, while she was there, she would check out a book on driving so that Daniel could have some of the technical knowledge of motor cars that might assist in his driving education.

For Daniel, the morning seemed to creep onward. He was learning from the lending staff who now seemed to embrace him more than before. He suspected that the Mountie joke had brought him into their professional brotherhood. Nonetheless, he was anxious over what the luncheon might tell him about his grandfather's code. Finally, Mr. Truesdale came by Daniel's chair and told him that Elizabeth had called and she was heading to the diner with interesting news. Daniel excused himself from one of the loan officers with whom he was working and left the bank with Mr. Truesdale. His level of excitement was increasing the closer he got to the diner. He wished that he had thought to ask Tess to join them but knew that her daddy was likely to accompany his great aunt from the library. After last evening's warning from Gus, he didn't wish to seem to ignore his concerns over their relationship.

Elizabeth and Gus greeted the two bankers with a smile and ushered them to a booth at the far end of the restaurant where they could talk in private. There Elizabeth handed Daniel the promised tutorial on driving that she had obtained from the library. They sat down and before the waiter brought water and menus, Elizabeth blurted out that they had reviewed several maps and feel that they have a good idea of the general location of the mine. Gus explained that the code gave the general vicinity but not the specific pinpoint of the position. He said that the code provided the degrees and minutes of latitude and longitude but not the seconds. Gus explained that navigation had become so sophisticated that the use of seconds could provide a much more accurate whereabouts than just degrees and minutes. Therefore, they were able to gather a general location from the code but not within a few miles. The country that held the mine was filled with streams and was heavily mountainous. While Gus was optimistic, he emphasized that it might take weeks or even months to comb the area where the mine might be. Even then, there was a chance that they might never find the gold in the rugged terrain.

Unbeknownst to the diners, Sargent Bigsby had walked into the front of the little café. He overheard some of the conversation regarding the words grandfather and treasure. Those terms peeked his interest and he tried to find a table near enough to hear their conversation but far enough away as to not be obvious. He was thinking to himself that the story he made up to try to cover his forgery might well be true. Maybe Daniel's grandfather was, indeed, a notorious gangster and bank robber.

Maybe he was alive and in cahoots with Daniel who was now working at a bank. It was all starting to make sense. If he played his cards right maybe he could still bring justice to the young foreigner who claimed Canadian citizenship and get a commendation or maybe even a promotion. He started dreaming about being asked to move up to Alberta or possibly Vancouver and have a real jumpstart to his career. Those big city Mounties had probably never busted a genuine bank robber so he would surely rise to prominence. Under any circumstances, however, he assured himself that he would keep a close watch on both Daniel and Tess.

Chapter Six: The Hunt is On

Daniel struggled through the rest of the week without seeing Tess. Her father had made sure she had plenty of errands to run and duties that would keep her busy in the evenings. To keep himself occupied, he recalled his aunt's offer for driving lessons and asked if she would teach him that skill. She owned an old Lincoln but also a snazzy Jeep convertible with manual transmission. After a few rough starts in the Jeep, Daniel started to get the hang of the interplay of clutch, gas, brake and shift. It was the hills that seemed to give him the most trouble. It took quite a few tries to keep from cutting the motor off or sliding backwards. Soon he finally developed the muscle memory of the precise combination of throttle and clutch release to move forward. He was proud of this new skill and the prospect of being able to use the Jeep to carry him in search of his grandfather's mine. Still he missed seeing Tess but, returning from lessons one evening, there was a note from her penned to his door. The note read,

"My dearest, I am sorry that my father has kept me under wraps this week. I know he thinks that he is doing the right thing but it only makes me want to be with you even more. Truly, absence makes the heart grow fonder. My heart aches to see you and the hours

until the weekend seem to be endless. Every night I have these marvelous dreams about us together and what our future holds.

I am so excited to do some hiking together on Saturday. I heard that you have a general location for us to start, however, Dad feels it will be like looking for a needle in a haystack. I don't care if we ever find any treasure, I just want to be with you and this is a great excuse for us to be alone. YOU are MY TREASURE! I just can't wait!!

All my love,

Tess"

Daniel was elated to read the passage and, mindful of his grandfather's enemies, hid the letter back down in the tunnel. He knew that the Mounties were not happy having him around but did not know who might be after his grandfather's money. Clearly, from his letter to Elizabeth, his grandfather was fearful of someone or some people that might be after his treasure. Daniel didn't want to have any evidence of treasure or gold that might be uncovered by antagonists known or unknown to him. He would have to be careful about himself and Tess.

The weekend finally arrived, and he asked Elizabeth to call Gus' home and see if Tess would like to come over for breakfast before heading off on their hike. She asked her father and received permission but gave her 'that look' that meant that he was wary of the two of them alone. He was about to suggest that he should probably come along as protection since bears would be trying to fatten up for the winter hibernation. His wife, however, gave him a similar look that halted his proposed intervention. He returned to his novel and Tess kissed him and her mother goodbye. She affirmed that she would be home in time for supper.

Back at Elizabeth's Daniel made sandwiches for their lunch and borrowed an old thermos jug to carry tea. Elizabeth gave him the keys to the jeep and a map of the area where she had marked a boundary of a few square miles where the letter had suggested the mine was located. She warned him to be careful since he didn't have his official driver's license and could be in trouble if he had a wreck. Soon thereafter, Tess arrived and greeted both with warm hugs and a quick kiss to Daniel. They sat down for a breakfast of blueberry pancakes, bacon and plenty of hot coffee. They ate quickly in their excitement to be alone and the prospects of a fun hike in the mountains. Before they left, Elizabeth handed Daniel a pistol that she explained had been left with her by his grandfather. She knew Daniel was familiar with firearms and warned him that bears were aggressive this time of year. Daniel agreed that anytime you go into the back country you need to be mindful of all the dangers – animal and human!

So, with full bellies and happy hearts they took off for their adventure into the woods and into life. They had barely gotten out of town before Tess kissed him on the cheek and placed her hand on his right thigh. The latter of those actions caused Daniel to swerve the jeep to the left which caused Tess to fall further into Daniel's side. Her natural reflex was to catch herself by pushing her hand to his left leg. This inadvertent move caused her palm to land squarely on Daniel's manhood. She quickly pulled back and flushed as she looked into Daniel's face to see if he was upset. Daniel's look was one of surprise which quickly turned into a smile as he recognized Tess's embarrassment. She apologized but was intrigued by what she had just felt. They both were of the age of hormonal urges that had yet to be satisfied and were eager to explore more of the opposite sex's hidden pleasures. To lighten the mood, however, every so often Daniel would jerk the car slightly to the left, sending Tess back toward him. They would both laugh but she kept her hands firmly in her lap.

Elizabeth's directions had placed them near the little town of Rossland a few miles west of Trail. The couple parked the car on the side of a dirt road, gathered their backpacks and headed up the mountainside. As they marched up the hillside, the enormity of their search became apparent. There were no marked trails, the area was heavily forested, and it was, as Gus had suggested, a bit like trying to find a needle in a haystack. Fortunately, Daniel had an excellent sense of direction and had thought to bring a compass, his firearm and plenty of tea to help avoid any dehydration. Before they got a hundred meters into the forest the couple stopped to enjoy a prolonged kiss. This would be continued virtually every few minutes or so as they climbed steadily upward. The forest seemed to surround them with aromatic green needles from the firs, spruces and pines while soft silent brown needles were felt underfoot. The terrain reminded him of home and for the first time in several weeks he missed his family back in Kaak. He wanted to tell them about all the changes in his life and vowed that soon he would ask his great aunt if he could drive back to his familiar home. Maybe he could even take Tess with him, although he doubted that Gus would permit her going into the United States. Perhaps Gus might go with them and have a reunion with Daniel's father. That would be nice.

As they climbed further upward and upward the couple encountered numerous streams which they tried to follow to see if there were any hidden mine potentials. All turned up negative as the couple explored diligently for any clues that could lead them to grandfather's gold. As they broke for lunch, they spread a blanket over a pinnacle that overlooked the valley and the Columbia River in the distance. It was a beautiful spot and allowed the couple time to relax with each other. After their lunch, Daniel sat on the blanket with Tess lying on her back with her head in his lap. As she looked up to him with the blue sky in the background, she felt she had never seen such a handsome man. It was not just that his features were attractive, it was his smile that really penetrated her mind. He just seemed so happy and carefree. She had lived a measured life of discipline and constraint. Daniel, on the other hand, just seemed to take life as it came. No agendas, No restraints. Just pure enjoyment of the moment. She wished she could be more like him, but if she couldn't, at least she could share his perpetual bliss.

Just as Daniel bent down to kiss her, they heard a banging sound. It was not a gun but sounded much more like a hammer hitting nails. Both wondered who would be up at this altitude building anything. They arose and followed the banging sound until they came to a small clearing. There they met an elderly gentleman who was working on repairing an old cabin. They introduced themselves and the gentleman explained that he had lived in the cabin when he was a young boy and hadn't visited the site for quite some time. He was a rather tall man with a large head but was so bent over from arthritis and the burdens of life, he appeared shorter than Daniel. He had nailed shut the door and indicated that he wanted to look inside for one last time. He was way too old to ever use the cabin again but had a sentimental attachment and wished to see where he grew up again.

Daniel asked what he planned to do with the cabin. The gentleman indicated that he hadn't really thought about that but suggested that he should probably sell the old place. It came with a deed for ten acres of worthless mountainside so it certainly wouldn't amount to much. Just as Daniel was in the midst of their discussion, Tess beamed up and said, "How much do you want for the place? I've got $500 I have that was designated for my college wardrobe. I think I can get by with the clothes I already have and we would surely like to own your cabin."

"Miss, I couldn't possibly ask that much for this run-down piece of history. I'm sure it is only valuable to my memory and I doubt I can make the climb up here again. I would just be happy to give you the property so you can enjoy it like I once did." Through all this Daniel was quiet, however, at the gentleman's offer, Daniel said it would be impossible to gift such a memory but would love to pay an agreed upon price - with the contingency that the gentleman could use it any time he felt up to making the climb. They made an agreement, shook hands and arranged to meet on Monday at the bank to change the title. The elderly man said he was pleased that his home and his memories would remain intact and would meet them to consummate the transaction. With that he bid the duo adieu and headed back down the mountain.

There was something about the old man that seemed somewhat odd. He had a certain look whenever his eyes met Daniel's. It was as if this meeting wasn't at all happenstance and his actions seemed almost rehearsed. It was hard to tell the height of the man since he was perpetually hunched over and his beard covered so much of his face it was hard to tell how old he might be. He didn't seem to be a menace but, at the same time he always seemed on guard. Perhaps he was just curious why a couple would be so far away from civilization with no marked trails. He seemed affable enough and interested in talking but sketchy about his past. He had introduced himself as J. Johns and he listened carefully when Daniel and Tess stated their names.

"Daniel," he replied when Daniel had introduced himself. "A good name. Nice to make your acquaintance."

Daniel and Tess were elated at this turn of events and took a quick tour of the insides of the little cabin. It was so small that it made Daniel's little cottage in his great aunt's back yard look like a plantation. There was only one room, a wooden table and sink and two bed frames. All seemed rather sturdy and the logs and fireplace made the cabin worthy of weathering the tough British Columbia winters. Just outside there was a giant tree with a girth at least of four meters. The tree conjured up Daniel's memory of his grandfather's tunnel and he vowed that, if he was going to continue his quest for the hidden mine, he would create a hidden way to escape his or his grandfather's enemies. The old tree might just provide such a getaway.

The remainder of the day they spent wandering about without much discipline in their search. The time slipped by quickly and their random kisses led way to wandering hands until they realized they needed to get back to the jeep and head back home. They certainly didn't want to be late and cause Gus to have further misgivings about their budding romance. They made it down the mountain and back into the jeep. Before they left, they kissed heavily and touched each other outside of their clothes until it was time to go. The gearshift made too much togetherness geographically impossible, however, Tess managed to tilt her head on his shoulder the whole way back to her house. Just before they arrived home she looked into the mirror to check her hair and makeup. No sense arriving to her parents looking like she had done just what she had done! As she anticipated Gus was waiting on the front porch when the couple arrived. Tess hopped out of the jeep and waved goodbye to Daniel and climbed the steps up to her father who smiled and likewise waved to Daniel.

Daniel had been dreading seeing Gus and it was quite a relief that he seemed ok with their all-day togetherness. As he was driving back to his cottage he started thinking about the events of the day. Certainly, he was excited about the little log cabin and the fact that it might provide him with some shelter while looking for the mine. He didn't have enough money to make the purchase by himself and had the foresight to think it might be best to put the ownership in Tess's name anyhow. If he became confounded by enemies of his grandfather, it might make a safe hideout that wouldn't have his name attached in any public record. He also reflected on the scope of their exploration. When he first arrived at the point at which they began the search, he was overwhelmed at the vast effort it would entail which might never reach fruition. He might waste all his time and come up empty. As he pondered that, he realized how much he enjoyed the outdoors and how enthralled he was to be literally 'walking in his grandfather's footsteps'. Plus, it didn't hurt that he could spend entire days alone with Tess. He resolved to spend some of tomorrow in the search.

Sunday morning, Tess and her family went to church but Daniel parked the Jeep in the same location as the day before. He felt he had had duplicate motives in yesterday's search. He mostly wanted to be with Tess and the surprise log cabin purchase blinded his logic of a scientific approach to combing the area. Today, he would start afresh proceeding up and down in a systematic fashion much like he did at Kaak when he wounded an elk. He would proceed as far as the map displayed at one end and return a hundred meters to the side of where he began the initial map line. This would be repeated until he had covered the entire area. He admitted to himself, in this rugged country, the task may not be completed for many weeks or even months. Even then, he was basing his efforts on an interpretation of a letter that may or may not have been a code. What if the whole effort was but a charade by his grandfather to confound anyone who might be attempting to find his treasure… if there really was any treasure to begin with? Even with these misgivings Daniel proceeded with the search, traversing up and down the mountains seeking any clues that might lead to whatever his grandfather had written about.

At the end of the day, Daniel headed back to Trail, exhausted, dirty and cut by briars along the way. Before he left the mountain, he noted the grid he had pursued as well as leaving a red bandana on a sapling to mark where he finished for the day. He returned to the cottage and took a much-needed shower. He was tired and hungry but most of all discouraged at the lack of progress from the day's efforts. Tomorrow, however, he would see Tess at the bank and would help with her purchase of the little cabin. Both events served to lighten his mood as did the portion of beef stew that Elizabeth had left for him. With a full belly, he fell asleep almost immediately after falling into his bed.

Monday morning found Daniel heading to the bank for work and away from his thoughts about hidden treasures. He had a job to do and was becoming exceptionally proficient at the lending process. His peers were pleased at how they had helped him learn the system and Mr. Truesdale was ecstatic at having a new officer that was affable with customers and confident enough to process loan requests expediently. He pulled Daniel aside during the morning and asked if he would like to come to dinner that evening. Daniel remembered that he had promised Mrs. Truesdale that he would dine with them every week, so he heartily agreed. During the morning, however, the elderly gentleman who owned the log cabin arrived and asked to see Daniel. At about the same time, Tess showed up and the three sat with the bank's notary and executed the sale agreement. Daniel explained to Tess that it would be better if the cabin was in her name since she would be paying the bulk of the purchase price, which they settled on $300. Daniel provided a bit from the savings from his last paycheck and promised Tess that he would pay her some amount each week to replenish her wardrobe account. She whispered to him that she didn't need ANY clothes when she was with him. The thought of which left him somewhat aroused as to her meaning and anxious over the next time they might be alone.

That evening Daniel walked over to Mr. and Mrs. Truesdale's home. They enjoyed a great dinner of elk steaks and root vegetables with banana pudding for dessert. Following dinner, Mr. Truesdale asked Daniel if he would have a glass of port with him and discuss some details of the bank. Daniel had never had port nor much of any alcoholic beverages before but to be polite he accepted. As they sat in the elder's study before the crackling fire, Mr. Truesdale asked Daniel how he was enjoying working in the lending function.

"I like it just fine, sir. My sister taught me well how mathematics was the only perfect science and my parents gave me a constant reminder to mind my manners and always use respect when dealing with people. The logic of mathematics together with empathy of understanding and meeting the needs of customers seem to be consistent features in making loans."

"I am glad to hear that." Spoke Mr. Truesdale. "I was afraid I was pushing you too hard and you might get burned out."

"Oh, no. I really enjoy the interaction of the finance and the understanding of the people who need money to build their homes or their businesses. It is fascinating to me and I feel that I am providing a valuable service to your bank and to its customers."

"OK, here is what I want to do my Mr. Daniel!" spoke Mr. Truesdale. "I want you to work with our maintenance supervisor and come up with a plan to build you out a private office. I think you are on a fast track that can really make a difference to our community. And, with your connections to Gus' family, you have an ability to provide a powerful ally for the bank."

"How is that Mr. Truesdale?" asked Daniel.

"You may not know this, but Gus has significant financial resources as well as relationships with influential people in political circles. Despite his rugged appearance, he is quite refined and knowledgeable on a variety of fronts. His connections on Wall Street, in Hong Kong and at the seat of government in Ottawa are extensive. He respects you and that can be what we need from our new loan officer. Right now, he has me in negotiations with a large rancher in Alberta to purchase land near Fort McMurray that holds a major position in the Athabasca Oil Sands. He doesn't have quite the capital to make the entire purchase, so the bank is willing to lend him the balance needed."

"Is this a promotion, sir?" questioned Daniel.

"You're damned right it is. I want you to start work tomorrow and get that office built. Don't worry about the other officers and any potential backlash. I know them and can explain your promotion in a fashion that should avoid any jealousies or animosities."

"Would it be OK if I asked Tess to assist me in the office build-out? She has design skills and it would be important to have her input. I know very little about construction and related activities and could surely create a real mess!"

"Fine, fine. Whatever you think is best. I will call her in the morning. It should make her AND her father happy that we are including them in this bank configuration."

Daniel thanked the Truesdales as he left to walk home. His mind was going in a thousand different directions as he thought about the treasure, Tess, the cabin, his new position and the new office. He was so distracted that he didn't notice the fact that he was being followed. As he made his way back home the shadowy figure stayed well in the background, but it was clear that Daniel was a target of some interest.

The next morning Daniel headed to the bank to meet with the maintenance supervisor to go over the broad outline of office construction that Mr. Truesdale had laid out. Together, they found the most likely spot and Daniel asked the supervisor if Tess could help with the design elements. The supervisor was more than happy to have someone else take on responsibilities. Like Daniel, he had little construction experience and was more into the maintenance aspect of his job. They finished their preliminary survey of the property just in time for Daniel to resume his banking duties at the opening of the doors. At lunchtime he walked over to Tess's house to tell her about his promotion and see if she would be interested in working on the office. She was pleased about Daniel's surprise visit and proud of his promotion as well as excited with the opportunity to apply her design skills. She accompanied him back to the bank and he showed her the general area where the office could be built. She made a number of sketches and promised to refine them into an architectural rendering.

On his way home from the bank he noticed a rugged looking individual that seemed to be trailing him. Daniel's experiences in the woods prepared him to recognize threats and this man looked like he knew his way around tracking. Daniel was apprehensive but didn't want his follower to know that he had been seen. Daniel headed straight to the cottage, giving no indication that anything had alarmed him. When he arrived home, he peeked out the window to see where the man had gone. Sure enough, the character was watching the cottage from a brushy vantagepoint. Daniel decided to turn the tables and went down the tunnel and emerged out of the tree stump. It was starting to become dusk, so he was not concerned about being seen in the old vacant lot. His plan was to circle around behind his stalker and perhaps track him to get an idea of where he was from. Daniel did not wish to confront the man. He simply wanted to get an idea of the potential threat and develop a defensive plan. He could only imagine that word of his arrival and relationship to his grandfather may have sparked interest from his grandfather's enemies. They must still be after their imagined treasure and Daniel's ability to lead them to whatever financial legacy his grandfather may have left. Daniel had turned no lights on in the cottage so eventually his rugged tracker gave up monitoring the house and left. Daniel's tracking skills were second to none and was able to follow the man to a part of town that was considered 'on the wrong side of the tracks'. He saw the man go into a shanty and was greeted by another equally scruffy individual. Daniel could not hear their conversation but knew it was about him. He made a mental note of the description of each man as he was sure he would encounter both at some future date. 'To be forewarned is to be forearmed', his father used to tell him, and he would have to use his wits to remain out of the clutches of his now known enemies.

As Daniel returned home, he decided to circle the block around his bungalow just to make sure that his followers weren't monitoring him in shifts. He worked his way completely around the cottage without seeing any prying eyes, so he went to the vacant lot, opened the stump hatch and entered the tunnel. He was happy that his grandfather had the foresight to create an ability to avoid being seen going in and out. His concern then turned to Tess. If questionable men were monitoring him, they could have hardly missed his relationship with her. He vacillated as to whether to tell her to be on-guard, which would certainly frighten her, or just be extra cautious whenever they meet up. He certainly didn't want anyone to know where she lives.

The next morning, he asked if he could use Elizabeth's telephone to call Tess and invite her to lunch at the diner to go over the renderings of his office. While he was anxious to start work on his office, this would allow him to check to see if she was already being followed. She said that she had worked on the drawings overnight and was excited to show him her work. At his suggestion they agreed to meet later than the normal lunch hour. That would allow him to slip out of the bank with another of the loan officers and go to a normal lunch. He could then shake any tail and follow Tess from her house to the diner and spot anyone that might be following her.

At noon, he asked if anyone wanted to go to have a quick lunch across the street at a hot dog vendor. One agreed and off they went. As they left the bank, Daniel surreptitiously scouted the area and didn't see anyone. Hopefully, that meant that he was not being watched during working hours and probably only when they thought he was looking for the hidden loot. As he finished lunch, he excused himself and took a zigzag route to Tess's home. Assured that he was not being followed, he wandered completely around the blocks surrounding her house. He was relieved that he didn't see any potential threat. He watched as she left home and headed straight for the diner. He stayed back a couple of blocks just to watch her progress and see if any tail might have picked her up. Again, there was no sign of anyone interested in her stroll to lunch. This made up his mind about not telling her about the events of the prior evening. No sense in jeopardizing their time together or have Gus involved. He could possibly ban the relationship outright if he felt that his daughter was subject to danger through her friendship with Daniel.

At lunch, they grabbed an out-of-the-way booth where they could both look at her work and steal a few subtle moments of intimacy. He was excited with her drawings and this was something that they could share together - building bridges in their professional endeavors as well as within the confines of their romantic lives. The mood was upbeat, and they made plans to meet again over the weekend and conduct a more systematic and orderly search of the mapped area. She said that her parents had to go out of town for the weekend so they could work both Saturday and Sunday. As they were leaving the diner, Daniel made an excuse to go to the bathroom and suggested she head home alone. They shared a quick but passionate kiss and she walked out the door and turned toward home. Daniel asked the waitress if he could use the delivery door in the back of the restaurant. She said that it was unlocked and would be fine, that other guests sometime used that as an exit. As soon as he went outside, he looked around to check if anyone might be watching. Having seen no one, he hurried around the diner to see if he could catch a glimpse of Tess's homeward journey. She was just crossing a street a couple of blocks away and didn't seem to have anyone interested in her walk. Daniel followed her, at a distance, all the way to her house. He then turned toward the bank to take Tess's drawings to the maintenance supervisor who would coordinate with the contractor.

That evening, instead of heading home, Daniel was picked up by Elizabeth who was to take him for his driving test. As he left the bank and into Elizabeth's jeep he spied the scuzzy character who greeted his follower of the prior evening. Evidently, they were working as a team to follow him only on his off-work hours. As Elizabeth drove off, Daniel watched as the man looked frustrated at this unexpected turn of events. He had expected to follow Daniel on foot and had no way to keep up with a motor vehicle.

Daniel passed his driving test and Elizabeth treated him to an ice cream cone at the local dairy mart to celebrate. Daniel was sure that it was his great aunt that really wanted an excuse for getting ice cream herself and interrogate him on Tess, the search and how things were going. He filled her in but also mentioned his desire to return to Kaak to visit his family. So much was going on in his life that he wanted to share with his kin. She agreed and volunteered to lend him the jeep any time. She had the old Lincoln that she felt safer in anyway and he needed the jeep to get to the search area.

During the rest of the week, Daniel was busy with the routine of banking and an occasional viewing of the progress on the office build out. Each evening when he went home, he would take the same route and act as casually as possible. He did not wish to have his trackers recognize that he was on to them. In fact, he tried to act as if he didn't have a care in the world but, also, didn't want them to think that he had already found the loot. He continued to dress the same, not spend money on any form of luxuries, including going out to eat. Knowing that they would be watching, he would leave his light on until about nine, turn out the light, then sneak out the tunnel to hunt the hunters. He wanted to know as much about them as he could before any confrontation might occur. For three nights he found where one of them would watch the house until about a half hour after the light went out then head back to his lair. Perhaps due to his youth, they made the mistake of underestimating Daniel and were becoming sloppy. Never did they choose a different viewing spot and even would light up a cigarette while they waited and watched. The lighted cigarette was like a beacon for Daniel and he had no trouble monitoring their set routine.

Finally the weekend arrived, and it was time to pick up Tess for their survey of the map. This time they would really focus on starting at the old cabin, find the bandana marking his previous search and crisscross the area until they found the correct stream. Daniel went to Elizabeth's house, made sandwiches and the thermos of tea and picked up the key to the jeep. Elizabeth kept the jeep in the attached garage and Daniel was careful that no one would see him opening the garage door and getting into the jeep. He took off in quite a rush and watched carefully in his rear-view mirror to see if he could spot either of the two threats. He did not see either but was aware that they might be observing his cottage and had not seen him enter Elizabeth's. In any regard, he made a circuitous route to Tess's home just to make sure he was not followed. When he arrived, Gus and his wife had already departed, and he and Tess were alone. She greeted him at the front porch and quickly ushered him into the house. There the two became locked in an unrestrained intimate interlude whereby clothing started falling on the floor. They were only half dressed when Tess suggested that they should probably stop and proceed with their original plan of searching for treasure. At this stage, all Daniel could think about was the treasures of Tess that lay within his grasp. It was hard for him to back off but respected her wishes and with deflated emotions began to gather his shirt and jacket. Fortunately, as other things started to deflate, his mind returned to the effort they must undertake.

At the search site, the couple laughed and giggled as they made their way to their now owned piece of property. They stopped there to drop off backpacks to lighten their load and speed up the exploration process. They agreed to split up and walk in parallel lines within hailing distance from one another. While they left the backpacks in the cabin, Daniel was careful to bring the loaded pistol and a box of ammo along for the hike. They hadn't traversed more than a couple of hundred yards when Daniel heard Tess cry out for help. He ran as fast as the difficult terrain would permit in the direction of Tess's shouts. He came upon her backing down a hillside, all the while facing a looming black bear. She was wise not to try to turn and run which would have only prompted the bear to view her as a food source. In an instant Daniel was by her side, pistol drawn. It was not necessary to pull the trigger either to frighten or kill the bear as the two human adversaries convinced the bear to seek alternate prey and he turned and ambled off. Tess's reaction reflected her adrenalin rush from fear and she collapsed into Daniel's arms. He held her tightly, all the while looking in the direction of the bear's departure.

He kept saying, "I am so proud of you. You did exactly what all the textbooks say and what any woodsman would recommend when dealing with bears."

As the adrenalin wore off, Tess's voice strengthened, "Thank you for coming to my rescue. I was afraid we might never finish what we started in my house this morning. If I was to die, I would surely have liked to experience the intimacy that I have never had, nor ever considered, until I met you."

She was shivering as they made their way back to the cabin. As she laid down on the cot, Daniel got a fire started and poured her a cup of tea. To some, the experience of life and death danger serves as an aphrodisiac and it was certainly the case with Tess. As she sipped her tea she asked Daniel to sit with her on the bed. She placed her head on his shoulder and sat down the cup. As they began to kiss, she slid her hand under his shirt and unbuckled his belt. Daniel began to pull up her sweatshirt above her head and unbuckle her bra. Unfamiliar with the hoops and catches of female lingerie and he made a mess of smoothly removing that part of her accouterments. Having failed at that, he quickly moved to her pants where he had measurably more success. Still locked in their kiss, except for socks, they were naked together. Without any hesitation Tess pushed him down and lay on top. They were still embraced in the same kiss and their eyes locked upon one another when lower bodies connected. Tess gave a gasp as he flowed into her entrance. By now kissing had stopped as both were panting from the exertion of lovemaking. As in most first lovemaking attempts, Daniel climaxed quickly, and the motions of his torso ceased. Tess, however, was still very much engaged in the act and continued her movements until her whole body shivered on top of

Daniel. As they both lay on the tiny cot, their kissing resumed, and it wasn't long before the couple became coupled again. This time the merger lasted for quite some time and, when both were satisfied, they fell asleep in each other's arms. When they awoke, it was late afternoon. They ate the sandwiches and began to slowly explore one another's bodies. It wasn't long before another wave of passion overtook the couple and lovemaking continued until it was late evening. The time had raced past their ability to prudently head back down the mountain in the dark. They decided the only course would be to spend the night and hike out in the morning. All discussion of treasure was dismissed as the treasures they had found in one another were more than sufficient.

Daniel took stock of their situation and looked around the cabin. There were no supplies of any kind nor was there any visible source of water. To have the cabin so long a habitat, Daniel figured that there must be some water nearby. After their lovemaking both wanted to freshen up and wash their faces. He took the flashlight out of the backpack and wandered around the outside of the house. Mindful of the proximity of the bear encounter, he took the pistol with him as he searched for some form of water. Near the back of the house he found what he was looking for – a small well that was overgrown by brush. Beside the well was a post and hanging on the post was a small bucket attached by a long cord. He looked down at the well and could see water below so, dropping the bucket, and pulling up the cord, he managed to fill half the bucket with sweet, cold water. He untied the bucket and carried it into the cabin.

Chapter 7

The following morning the couple resumed their search. With the prior bear encounter fresh in their minds, they stayed together this time and kept a watchful eye for any possible threat. After several miles of walking, the couple came across several small springs that merged into little streams. Each time they found a creek, their excitement rose. But each time their hopes were dashed as they followed the stream to its source without uncovering any potential mine. On a couple of occasions, Daniel would take out his pan from the backpack and scoop up some of the sand and silt from the creek bottom. He would spin the mixture in the flowing water and look for any telltale signs of a glint in the sunlight. Having no success, the couple continued their quest until midday. Since they consumed all their provisions the day before and had expended considerable energies in lovemaking and hiking, they were famished. They agreed to return to the jeep and head home.

Daniel was extremely cautious as he approached Tess's house. He knew that his 'watchers' had noticed the jeep and would be on the lookout. Having seen no one as he entered the town, he dropped off Tess and told her he would return on foot. He made up a tale that Elizabeth might need the jeep and that was the reason for not staying. He returned to the garage and slipped into his cottage.

He showered and changed clothes and looked out the window to see if his two antagonists were watching the house. He started thinking of them as Frick and Frack, the Swiss comedy skaters that performed slapstick routines for the Ice Capades. Fortunately, it didn't appear as if he was being monitored so he left the normal way but proceeded to Tess's in a circuitous route that would ensure he was not leading anyone to her home. Tess had also cleaned up and made sandwiches for the couple. Both ate hungrily and discussed the lack of traction in their search. Daniel started thinking about his grandfather's letter and decided that he would re-read it to see if there were any hints that might provide a more accurate location for their continued search. Knowing that Tess's parents could show up at any time, Daniel thought it prudent to head back home and leave Tess to greet them alone.

Back at the cottage Daniel caught sight of Frick or Frack loitering around the neighborhood. Taking care to not be seen, he knocked on his great aunt's front door and was let in by Beatrice. She explained that Elizabeth had taken the jeep to get some groceries and gasoline. Oops, he thought; He should have been considerate enough to fill the tank before he returned. He would surely make amends next time he saw her. He exited out the back door and quietly slipped into the cottage unaware that while Frick might not have seen him, Frack was at the opposite side of the yard and most certainly saw Daniel's arrival. As soon as Daniel entered the cottage he opened the trap door and pulled out the letter. He carried it over to the kitchen table and carefully read the document, careful to spot any irregularities that might be a clue. He read and re-read the letter before noticing that the words 'post' and 'well' were in all capital letters. Thinking that was the only aberration in the physical review of the letter he began saying the words over and over. Did 'post' mean letter or a wooden stake? Did 'well' refer to a place where water is dug from the ground or does it refer to something that is positive. He turned these possible clues over in his mind but could not make any sense that they could help him locate the mine.

He was exhausted so he returned the letter back to a hidden spot in the ladder of the tunnel and climbed into bed. That night he had a marvelous dream about Tess and the romantic interlude that they had experienced over the weekend. When he awoke, however, his dream led him to recall the old well outside the little cabin that they had purchased. When he was looking for a way to draw water from the well there was a bucket on a post. Perhaps the 'post' and 'well' clues were right in front of him all the time! In his excitement he rushed off to work that morning with a determination to head to the cabin as soon as possible. He would have to ask Elizabeth if he could borrow the jeep again and apologize for not gassing it up when he returned it. He wouldn't tell her or anyone about his theory on the words. No need in building up hopes if the course proved to be a dead-end.

Work was being conducted on his new office, so it was not unusual for Tess to drop by to check on its progress. As she entered the bank, Daniel greeted her warmly but not so warm as to start tongues to wag among the bank staff. Mr. Truesdale, likewise, engaged her in conversation about her parent's weekend trip and suggested that she and Daniel have dinner at his home during the week. Both agreed to the invitation and Daniel left Tess to consult with the builder and maintenance supervisor. It was extraordinarily difficult for Daniel to focus on work with his mind (and body) completely fixated on looking at Tess. Where once she was simply an attractive young lady, now she had become a precious part of his life and future. It is said that 'love captivates' and in Daniel's case the captivation was an eagerly willing donation of a part of his soul.

After work, Daniel headed to his cottage to clean up before walking over to see if Tess might be interested in talking about furnishings for his new office. As Daniel left the cottage, he looked at the normal spot where his shadows normally hid. He didn't see anyone, so he left out the front door. Regrettably, Frick was running late for his surveillance duties and had not reached his traditional viewpoint. Unfortunately for Daniel, however, he was just in time to catch Daniel's departure. Unaware that he was now being shadowed, Daniel hastily walked toward Tess's home. About that time Sargent Bigsby was making his rounds. He happened to see Daniel leave and thought he might just monitor this would-be bank robber. As he laid back, he happened to notice that he was not the only person interested in Daniel's movements. Frack had joined up with Frick and together they were obviously trailing Daniel. Bigsby thought to himself that these were surely not a member of any gang that Daniel might have employed but, perhaps, they knew of a bank heist and wanted to keep a close eye out for an opportunity to rob the robber. Bigsby was beside himself with excitement as he was one step closer to cracking the case that hadn't happened. He made a quick mental note of the two suspicious characters descriptions and continued to follow the trio.

Daniel knew that he was an obvious target of the Frick and Frack crew and had maintained caution. Since the days when he was trailed by the wolfpack back in Kaak, he developed a sixth sense that could almost feel when danger lurked from behind. As he walked on, he tried to notice if he was being tailed. Once when he turned a corner that had a high hedge, he slid within the hedge and waited. His instincts proved accurate as his two antagonists cautiously turned the corner and then sped forward as their target was no longer in sight. They reached the corner of the next block and one went left and the other went right. Quickly, Daniel pushed through the hedge and directly into Sargent Bigsby who had also just turned the corner. The two glared at each other but the Mountie tipped his hat and Daniel excused himself. Daniel went back to his cottage as Bigsby continued to walk toward the intersection of the next block. Looking both ways, the lawman could not see either of the two trackers, so he continued his rounds. He was, however, aware that Daniel knew he was being tailed and people are followed only if there is jealousy or money involved. Certainly, neither Frick nor Frack were jealous husbands bent on extracting revenge on some spurious affair. No, they were there clearly in the hopes that Daniel would lead them to a treasure or some treasure yet to be acquired.

At the bank the following morning two incidents would catapult Daniel's lending career. The first was a closing on the largest loan in the bank's history. Part of the Canadian contribution to the Manhattan Project was that the Cominco institute, located in Trail, produced electrolytic heavy water. In doing so the environment was slowly being impaired and Cominco needed capital to clean up the toxic byproduct. The manager of the plant had met Daniel when he was in the teller line needing some ledger-book reconciliation. The manager appreciated the assistance and asked for Daniel when he needed to apply for credit. Daniel completed all the documentation and analysis of the credit, and the loan closing went perfectly. Daniel had to call in the lead loan manager to finalize the deal because the hypothecated amount exceeded Daniel's lending limitation.

The second incident regarded the recovery of a loan that had gone bad. In the book that Mr. Truesdale had lent Daniel, Daniel read about a number of tools that could help in mitigating loan losses. One that he recalled was to utilize existing unencumbered capital assets to factor the payoff of tenuous loans. It just so happened that a land management company had become overextended on operating capital and was on the verge of defaulting on a rather hefty property loan. Daniel worked with the officer on that account to review the real estate assets of the management company and found that the value of the real estate had not taken into account the considerable timber holdings on the property. Consequently, the re-evaluation allowed for the creation of a second mortgage based upon this unrecognized value which allowed the favorable closing on the note to the bank.

Mr. Truesdale was delighted at Daniel's ability to think through both problems and opportunities to arrive at solutions for customers and the bank. In one day, Daniel had saved the bank millions from a loan loss and had produced many thousands in fees and interest from the Cominco loan. He asked Daniel to join him in his office at the close of business.

Truesdale said, "Take a seat Daniel. I want to talk about today and your tomorrows. I have decided to open a branch in Castlegar about 30 kilometers north of here. I have asked our senior lending officer to be the president of that new venture and he has accepted. Therefore, I want you to assume his role here as the head of our lending operations."

"Sir." said Daniel, While I am honored that you have that much faith in me, aren't there other lenders that have significantly more seniority than me?"

"Perhaps so, but you are clearly more engaged and have a natural feel for the whole process from A to Z. I would be around to watch over you and field any questions that you might have. I would also propose we give you a $1 million lending authority, the move to your new office and a significant pay raise. So? What do you think?"

"Well, sir. I can hardly turn that down. Now I can repay Tess for the cabin we purchased and have some cash to refinish the place."

"Speaking of Tess. I might even be willing to let you have an occasional Friday off to visit her when she starts college this fall. I hear you two are getting along quite well."

Daniel blushed at the reference but suddenly saddened by the reality that his love would be away from him shortly. Mr. Truesdale's comment was something he had placed in the back of his mind but, ultimately, he would have to face the fact that Tess would be leaving Trail. He vowed to spend as much time in the next few weeks with her as possible. He would have to negotiate between the Frick and Frack tail, the Mounties and Tess's father in order to see her safely.

The next morning Tess thought she would surprise Daniel with a homemade breakfast. She arose early and pack smoked salmon, croissants from the downtown bakery, coffee and boiled eggs. As she neared Daniel's cottage, she noticed a rather scruffy looking individual that seemed to have no place to go and was just standing around. She thought that odd, however continued onto the lawn and knocked on the door. As Daniel opened the door, he uttered exclamation of surprise but hurriedly begged her to enter quickly. Somewhat taken aback by his abrupt behavior, her concerns were relieved when he placed a passionate kiss on her lips. As the embrace ended, he peeked out the window where his watchers normally placed themselves only to see Sergeant Bigsby having a rather heated discussion with Frick. Perhaps Frick was too busy with the discussions to have noticed Tess's arrival, but Daniel couldn't take that to chance. He sat down and explained the clue that he had uncovered from the original letter. While that interested her, she noticed a defined change in Daniel's demeanor.

"Is everything OK?" She asked. "You don't seem excited about this new possible hint."

"You are perceptive. I need to tell you that it appears that my grandfather's enemies have found out about me and have been hanging around for a couple of days. Nothing threatening, but I have been being followed by two questionable characters have been worried that you might become a target as well."

"A target of what?" she exclaimed. "I'll have you know I can take care of myself. Particularly with an oaf like the one I just saw."

"I'm sure you are very capable, but these men are desperately interested in grandfather's treasure and, maybe, they could have been the cause of his disappearance. We just can't be too careful. They might try to kidnap you and hold you for a ransom that I can't afford unless we do find the gold mine. I truly love you and would like to spend the rest of my life with you in my world."

Daniel's honest proclamation of love came as such a surprise that Tess was shocked into silence. Only a single tear of joy decried her feeling of complete and utter happiness. She, too loved Daniel but had been somewhat reticent to proclaim her compete infatuation with every aspect of Daniel's being.

"Oh, my darling. You must know that I am in love with you too. I also believe we have a future together." At that comment, breakfast, gold and antagonists were forgotten as the couple melted into each other on the floor of the happy little cottage.

When they finished making love, Daniel told her of Mr. Truesdale's decision regarding the new promotion to Senior Loan Officer. She was delighted and suggested that she make a celebratory cake for when they have dinner at the Truesdale's. Daniel agreed, just as long as the cake has gold colored icing! He insisted that he escort her out the front door just in case Frick had noticed her arrival. He didn't want to allow for any speculation about a secret exit that might be essential for him in the future. As the couple left, neither Frick nor Frack were visible, probably as a result of Sargent Bigsby's tongue-lashing.

Irrespective of not seeing any of his trailers and not wanting to take any chances, Daniel walked Tess around for several blocks in the opposite direction of her home. Feeling that they were not being followed, Daniel chaperoned her to her house. Gus was sitting on the front porch and asked Daniel if they had made any progress on the search. Now that the cat was out of the bag on his interpretation of the post and well clue, Daniel explained his theory about the post at the old well behind their cabin. In a gesture of good will, Daniel invited him to accompany the couple back to the cabin on Saturday morning and test his notion.

That week, the Truesdale's fulfilled their promise of a celebratory dinner for Daniel and his new appointment. To further make the dinner festive, they invited Gus and his wife as well as Elizabeth to attend.

"I'll have you know that our Mr. Daniel has developed into a real superstar in our bank." Mr. Truesdale told the assembled party. He went on to explain how Daniel had made a huge loan and, at the same time, saved a precarious lending situation.

"Just this week, I promoted him to our Senior Lending position and will move him into his new office next week. Tess has done a masterful job in fully integrating the office structure in an unused part of the bank and I have decided that it will be a prototype for our new facility that I am opening in Castlegar."

While Tess and Daniel were both glowing under Mr. Truesdale's praise, you could tell that Gus was proud of his daughter's accomplishment and, to a certain extent, of her choice in male acquaintances.

Mr. Truesdale produced a bottle of champagne to celebrate the occasion. Daniel had never tasted the bubbly wine and was a bit unsure of whether he liked it or not. After a couple of glasses, however, and another bottle produced, he decided it wasn't too bad. The evening was filled with laughter at the tales that both Gus and Mr. Truesdale told of their careers and adventures of their extraordinary lives. Finally, Tess provided the gold iced cake that she had baked especially for the occasion. All were in a festive mood when they left the Truesdale home.

Early Saturday morning, the sky had darkened and a thunderstorm unleased a huge torrent of rain on the little Jeep with Gus, Tess and Daniel crammed inside. Knowing that the trail would be slick and dangerous for both Tess and her father, Daniel suggested that he go alone up to the cabin and review the post. He brought Gus' shovel in case any markings on the pole were not evident and it was set soundly into the ground. The going proved tough and slippery but after forty-five minutes of arduous climbing, Daniel made it to the cabin. Daniel went inside to both reminisce on his first taste of physical love and to dry off a bit before checking out the post. He tried to recall every detail of their encounter and found himself sweating and his heart pounding with each recollection. Finally, he put back on his poncho and headed to the backyard. There stood the post as he remembered. This would either be a wasted effort, or it could be just the sign that could lead him to the hidden mine.

He carefully scanned the post as it stood in the ground. The bucket was still affixed by the rope which Daniel untied earlier when they needed to freshen up. He walked around the post several times looking for any carvings or other indications that might be informative. It was difficult to see in the heavy downpour so he tried to push over the pole. In the soaked soil he could feel it giving away and after a few attempts on several sides, he managed to push it over. It was about six feet from tip to tip and not particularly heavy. To get it down the mountainside in this slippery terrain, however, might prove considerably difficult. In a sagacious moment, he decided to bring the bucket and use its rope to pull the pole behind him down the mountain.

He started down the hillside with the pole in tow and holding the bucket. Unfortunately, his sagacious moment turned inside out as the post slid past him, pulling him fifteen meters or so before he could regain his footing. So, if this is the way it's going to be, Daniel thought to himself, I will just let the post and its message help me down. Hanging onto the rope, he let the pole slide down the slope and tried to guide it from tangling in the brush or hit any of the many tree trunks on the way down. When he reached the bottom, Tess and Gus were still in the warm dry car.

"Oh, my gosh, what is that?" Declared Tess as she witnessed the pole come sliding down onto the road in front of them.

At the very moment that Gus looked up, he saw Daniel sliding down, hanging on the rope and covered in mud and leaves.

"Well, I guess that's our boy!" He uttered.

Eager to join them, Daniel knocked on the window which Gus rolled down in his laughter at the sight of the mud man outside. However, he immediately donned his poncho and came out to help load the post on the luggage rack above the Jeep's cab.

On the ride home Gus asked Daniel if he could see anything on the post that might confirm his hypothesis on the clue. Daniel replied that he couldn't spot anything in the bad weather but when they returned to Trail, they could examine the pole in more detail. Surely, Grandfather wouldn't leave any obvious directions that would allow his mine to be easily discovered. When they arrived at Gus' rental, they unloaded the post on the front porch and went inside to dry off. Daniel was soaked to the skin so Gus offered him some of his dry clothes. Gus was a much bigger man than Daniel, so he looked like a hobo with pants rolled up and shirt three sizes too big. Nonetheless, Daniel was happy to be warm and dry again and was eager to examine the chunk of wood on the porch. They brought out a flashlight and a magnifying glass to examine for any indication of writing or carving. Tess held the light while Daniel peered through the glass and Gus slowly turned the post. The initial screening did not turn up anything other than a normal round pole. However, below the dirt line, the smoothness of post changed. There were numerous scratches and small holes. The holes were probably as a result of underground creatures that gnaw on wood for either food or lodging. There was an area that seemed to have a marking but was covered with mud from the mountain sliding episode. They quickly brought a bucket of water and a brush to clean off the section. Sure enough there was a small carving on the side of the wood. It said only, '300s'.

"That's it?" Exclaimed Tess! "What does that mean? Three hundreds of what?"

"I don't know," Daniel returned. "The important fact is that this is obviously from Grandfather and the clue within the letter is accurate. He did, indeed, mean for us to use the capital letters of 'well' and 'post' as part of the maze of finding his mine. Everything is in riddles as he had really tried to avoid anything regarding the location of the mine falling into the hands of his enemies."

"Perhaps we are reading this all wrong." Interjected Gus. "Instead of this being the plural of 300, maybe it is 300 of some measure to the South." That would be just ambiguous as to not attract attention as a direction to his mine, but a large enough clue that, together with the letter, we could find his mine. If he is, indeed, trying to lead us, he must presume we are really quite perceptive. I wonder if he is maybe still out there watching our progress and, helping us along. I have a more than strong feeling that his demise may be just a perception that he has tried to engender to throw off any of his antagonists."

"Gosh, that makes perfect sense." Said Tess. "But what might be the measurement of the 300? Three hundred meters South, or feet, or what?"

"Well, it is certainly not kilometers or miles. It is most likely meters, yards or feet." Said Gus. "Remember, your grandfather grew up using both the metric system as well as the English Imperial system. I think, however, we can probably also rule out feet as you have already scanned the area that close to the cabin."

"So, when the weather clears up, let's take a compass and a measuring tape and try to narrow down our search." added Daniel.

Rain continued throughout the week and it wasn't until Saturday that the sky cleared and presented a

crystal-clear morning. Daniel was eager to continue
to utilize this latest clue but was afraid that he was
getting so close that his watchers might just close in
on him. He decided to leave the cottage just as the
sun rose but exited utilizing the underground tunnel.
He was careful not to raise the stump fully until he
had scanned the perimeter of the vacant lot. He
popped out and headed to Gus' house careful to
watch for any sign that he was being tailed. He made
a loop around the block as he approached the house
just as an extra precaution.

Since it was an early hour, he would not wake the
family and he could wait on the front porch. He
needn't bothered for when his foot hit the first step,
Gus was opening the front door and begged him to
enter. It was readily apparent the Gus had every
intention of accompanying the couple in this,
hopefully, last search. He was already dressed in high
boots, waxed pants, windbreaker and his 44-caliber
revolver was strapped to his side.

" I hope you don't mind if I come along," Gus
stated with a sheepish look. "I am just thrilled by the
hunt and was hoping I could assist in some way. I
know this is your venture and I may be stepping out
of my bounds but I am just so excited about finding
your grandfather's legacy."

Daniel had plenty of experiences with taking dogs on
hunts. They get so anxious when they see the hunter

gather his gun and equipment. It is a feature that is bred into true hunting dogs. When, however, the dog is left back or, worse yet, not included to go with other dogs, the sadness in the dog's face is pronounced. Unless you want to have a howling dog or a disappointed friend, best to have them accompany any such hunt. It was that same 'hound-dog' look that Gus gave Daniel as he let his expression beg to be a part of this adventure.

"Of course, you can come. You have been a part of this from the very beginning and now that we may be closing in on the riddle how could you be excluded?" exclaimed Daniel. Even though Daniel was expecting to have Tess alone to himself today, he could hardly express that to Gus.

About that moment Tess made her entrance and, seeing her father all decked out as if he were a part of the 'Charge of the Light Brigade', she cried out, "And what, my dear father, are you dressed to do today? I don't think Mom was expecting you to go clothes shopping with her and her friends?"

"Ahh, I was just thinking that you might need a hand today. It is going to still be slippery going and who knows what you might run into up there. You already told me about the bear situation, and you might need a strong arm if you find something that needs carrying down."

Daniel was thinking about the people that have been obviously tailing him and whether he should let Gus know or not. On one hand, if he spills the beans, he might lose Tess as her father might ban the two simply due to the perceived danger of their relationship. On the other hand, if he failed to warn Gus, and something happened to Tess, he would never forgive himself. His love was pure so he decided to take a chance and tell Gus everything.

"Tess, Gus is right. I think he needs to know that I have noticed, on several occasions, that someone was watching the cottage or trying to follow me. I am sure there are two of them and they look like just the type of ruffians that my grandfather feared. I didn't raise any alarms until I confirmed my apprehensions, but, once I saw Mountie Bigsby questioning one of the two in an agitated fashion. Perhaps the Mountie's confrontation was sufficient to send the two on their way, however, they seem such desperate men that a mere verbal warning wouldn't have much effect."

"Thank you for letting me know, Daniel. I too have noticed a couple of unsavory characters in areas where it would be odd to find them just hanging around. You can't be too careful and that's another reason why I am happy to be involved. Tess means everything to me, and I will do anything to protect her. I have come to trust you, Daniel and think that you only want the best for her. Together we will find that dad-burn treasure, and if anyone gets hurt in the process, it won't be us!"

Tess recognized her father's braggadocious behavior. She had seen it in the past and generally ignored it, however, was happy that her father seemed to really like Daniel. She had been apprehensive of her father's acceptance of the relationship and now was elated that it didn't appear that he would be an impediment to their affair.

"Ok, let's get started!" exclaimed the excited Gus. "We can take my car. I already have the shovel, a measuring tape and a compass. I think we should move the post off the front porch and put it in the garage where we can lock it up."

Daniel smiled at Gus' eagerness and was pleased that Gus took the report on Frick and Frack without undue apprehension.

The trio climbed into the van and took off for the mountains. Gus' wife had made sandwiches the night before and left them in the refrigerator. Apparently, Gus had already decided that he would be included in the exploration! Daniel had to smile to himself at Gus' presumptions but was glad to have some assistance and a comrade in case his watchers become aggressive.

As they parked the car, they were careful not to leave it in an obvious location close to where they would initiate the search. A quarter mile of hiking on the flat road would not be too much of a caution at this stage of their quest. They climbed the hill in the same spot that Daniel had made his glorious slide the previous weekend. Nothing seemed out of the ordinary and it was a glorious late summer morning in British Columbia. They reached the cabin and dropped off their backpacks and lunch. From where the post was removed from the well-head, Gus took a bearing due south with his compass. From there Daniel took one end of the tape measurer and walked in as straight a line as the terrain would permit. It wasn't at all easy to keep a reasonably direct course through the forest and rocky landscape. At the end of the fifty-yard tape Daniel drove a stake into the ground and hollered for Gus and Tess to join him. There, Gus would take another bearing and the process was repeated until they had reached 300 yards. The fact that, at exactly that point, they had uncovered a small stream served to heighten their excitement.

Daniel took his gold pan from their tools and swished some of the stream's sand around. Nothing appeared to be gold from this first endeavor. Daniel would repeat the exercise five or six more times before becoming a bit discouraged. Tess suggested that they look around for the source of the stream since their calculations were a bit by the 'seat of the pants' and, she recalled that they didn't know whether the distance would be measured in yards or meters. When she suggested this, Daniel and his math skills quickly recalibrated the distance to 274 meters. They agreed to expand the search by another 26 yards and spread out to see if this held any better promise.

The trio spread out with Tess and her father going a bit east and Daniel a bit west in an arc so as to stay around the 300-meter distance from where the post once stood. Apparently, the stream that they had found curved and its head waters were derived from a small underground culver where water bubbled out of the ground. Tess was the first to spot the exact location and yelled for Daniel to join them. As the threesome climbed down to the culver there was no indication of any sort of cave entrance or sampling of gold dust in the sand surrounding the creek. They looked everywhere in the general vicinity of the culver to no avail. There was simply no sign of a depression or any other clue that would imply that there was a mine shaft hidden away there. In fact, the only sign of any human exposure was a chewing tobacco tin that was half sunk into the culver.

Disappointed, the trio stopped to reconsider the clues and to rest a bit from their adrenaline-fueled search. Tess, however, walked back to the culver and fished out the tobacco tin. As she scraped the mud off the lid, she saw the embossed cap said, "Gold Dust Tobacco Company - The World's Finest Chew! She literally shrieked when reading the words. Gus and Daniel were with her in a moment and Daniel tried to pull off the cap from the body of the tin. Apparently, it had been glued shut. Gus took his knife out and began to pry open the lid. As the lid gave way a simple piece of canvas fell on his lap.

Chapter 8

While Daniel and Gus were busy unfolding the canvas, Tess took a good look at the metal container. She felt it odd that the metal was shiny and looked relatively new. If it had been in the weather and mud for very long, the metal would have lost its luster. Yet in the break in shadows cast by the canopy of leaves, the sun reflected the a bright sheen of the can. It was hardly placed there too long ago.

Meanwhile, the canvas was unfolded and spread out on the forest ground. In handwritten print, were the words, "Tarry not, the wind sits on the shoulder of your sail. Return to the mast at your purchase. At the cleat your quest will be completed."

The hair on Tess's arm began to rise as she understood the implications of the can and the comment on the canvas. She immediately looked around to see if there was anyone watching, for she now knew that all their efforts had been monitored. Someone was directing their activities and she had a fear that it was not necessarily for the positive. Clearly, this was not something that Daniel's grandfather had put together a long time ago and sent the letter to Elizabeth to help find his treasures. Perhaps Gus was right that Grandfather was indeed alive and 'prompting' their search. Equally likely, however, was the prospect that evil men were luring them into a trap!

She exclaimed, "Don't you see. We have all been being manipulated like puppets on a string. This can is new, it could not have been placed here by your grandfather long ago. The fact that someone knows that we have purchased the old cabin is proof that we are being controlled."

"Tess, dear. I think that you are both right and wrong, said her father. Yes, someone is playing a game with us, for what reason I can only guess. However, I think that we know who this person is and the whole effort is but a ruse to keep Daniel's grandfather's message as secretive as possible. Remember when I told you about your grandfather's experiences at sea. If you read the words on the canvas, the first sentence is from Polonius' advice to Laertes just before he set sail for France. The reference to 'sail' and 'mast' and 'cleat' are all nautical terms with which your grandfather would be familiar. No, I think that the old gentleman you met here on the mountain and sold you the cabin was, indeed, Daniel's grandfather. Remember, we only thought he had passed due to his disappearance and Elizabeth's fears. We knew he had enemies, is probably too old to work any mining venture and wanted his only grandson to reap his legacy."

"Oh, my goodness," exclaimed Daniel. He was elated with the prospect that his relative might still be alive and pointing the way to his fortune. "Let's

go back to the cabin and see if we can find a mast
and a cleat. Perhaps, he is there now and waiting for
us to unlock all these mysteries."

They were careful on the return to the little cabin.
They figured since his grandfather was so paranoid
about his enemies, they must represent a bigger
threat than just Frick and Frack. The two dunces
were probably just paid thugs to keep an eye on
anything in Trail that might lead to grandfather or
his gold. Greater foes must be behind grandfather's
fears. They cautiously reconnoitered the area around
the cabin as they made their final approach. Nothing
seemed out of the ordinary, so they went inside.
They made a through search of the cabin's insides
and saw no mast or cleat. Given the hidden tunnel
under the floor of Elizabeth's cottage, they made
special attention to any loose floorboards. They
found nothing in the cabin, however, that looked
like or pointed toward the items mentioned. When
they went outside they focused on the huge tree that
was close to the house. It was not only wide but also
very tall and very straight. Gus was the first to notice
that the only limbs of the tree were about fifty feet
up and completely opposite one another much like
the spars of old sailing ships.

"Aha", remarked Daniel as he gazed up to the
branches. "This must surely be the 'mast' of the
note. Let's see if we can find a 'cleat'.

Almost immediately Tess pointed upward about ten feet to a metal cleat imbedded into the tree. It had been painted to match the bark and would not be readily visible unless someone knew exactly where to look and what to look for.

"Ok, so this is obviously something to do with the mine or hidden gold or some treasure. But what?"

Daniel recalled how his grandfather had used the old stump as an escape hatch from his tunnel at the cottage. Perhaps this followed the same strategy. He began looking carefully at the bark below the cleat. After close inspection he noticed minute cuts running down the bark in parallel lines about two feet apart. As he touched the area nothing seemed to respond, and nothing seemed different from any other part of the tree. He decided that he should climb up to the cleat and inspect it more carefully. He took a line from his pack and tossed it across the cleat and was about to use it to shimmy up the tree. As soon as he added pressure on the line, however, the tree opened a gap where the parallel cuts had been. Much like the cantilever of some doors, the cleat had served as a pivot to open a hollow in the trunk of the tree. Daniel was so surprised that he let go of the line and the bark 'door' immediately closed, leaving the tree exactly as it had been before.

"Gus, would you get me a flashlight from your pack so we can see what is within the tree trunk?" asked

Daniel. "I will open it again and see if you can train your spotlight on the insides."

Sure enough, as soon as Daniel pulled the line the bark door opened once again, and Gus's spotlight revealed a ladder going down below the tree. Daniel noted that he could hold open the door with his hands even if he removed the loop from the cleat. Tess and her father climbed down and announced that there was a tunnel at the bottom of the ladder. Daniel started down the ladder but not before closing the door behind him, leaving no trace of their entrance.

Upon further investigation, the tunnel turned out to have several branches outward from a center circle of about ten feet. There were numerous pieces of mining equipment and chunks of discarded ore on the floor of the cavern. None of the ore showed promise of having traces of gold so the three started down one of the tunnels. Gus trained his spotlight on the walls and the floor of the shaft to expose any sign of gold. The shaft only ran about ten yards before making a right turn. That corridor extended another ten or so yards before coming to an abrupt stop. Evidently, this borehole had turned up empty. The threesome retraced their steps back to the spoke of the several shafts. They made their way down another tunnel with no more success than the first. On their third venture, however, the flashlight revealed several sparkles that might be dust or tiny nuggets.

Gus remarked, "Now we are starting to get some show. These reflections are most likely tailings and may have given some hope to your grandfather that the effort may be worthwhile. There is the end of the shaft, so my guess is that he ran another tunnel near this one to see if there was any vein."

Sure enough, the next tunnel they entered was extra wide, much like something found in the pictures of old mines out west. As they proceeded along the excavation, the angle of the shaft started downward. Again, this looked optimistic to the threesome as if the miner was following a vein that wandered deeper. Gus, who had more experience with mining, explained to his daughter and Daniel that veins of gold generally are relatively small, usually only a few inches wide, but can run for a couple of hundreds of yards in length. Generally, they are found alongside quartz or other hard minerals to breakthrough with traditional pick and shovel. The sheer magnitude of grandfather's effort was amazing. As they reached the end of the tunnel, Tess exclaimed, "Look, there is a circle of gold in the middle of the wall!"

"Wait, that is just the end of a vein and is really a tube that looks to be pretty pure gold," noted her father.

Daniel ran back to the main cavern and grabbed a pick. When he brought it back and took a hard swing at the yellow ore, a significant piece of gold and quartz hit the floor. They scrambled to examine the chunk and noted the heft of the golf-ball size piece of ore. While they were excited over their find, they agreed to continue to explore the other two shafts. The other tunnels showed some tailings but nothing like a vein that represented potential. Evidently, grandfather had tried several exploratory tunnels before finding a vein that had yet to be exploited fully. It was impossible to determine where the vein had started and how far along will it end.

They noted the late hour and agreed to drive back to Trail and have their find assayed. They would be careful to avoid any local rumors on a potential gold find in the area so decided to have it taken to a larger city that wouldn't raise any questions.

The threesome returned to Trail in a buoyant mood. The atmosphere of the evening, however, dampened when they stopped off at Elizabeth's home. When she answered the door, tears were pouring down her cheeks and she ushered them in quickly.

"What has happened Aunt Elizabeth? are you OK?"

"I am fine, however you should come quickly to meet your grandfather!"

"What, my grandfather is here?"

"Yes, but not for long I fear!" returned Elizabeth.

"What does that mean? Does he have to leave before we can learn about him and his life?"

"Just follow me upstairs," she blurted through her tears.

At the first bedroom at the top of the stairs was the elderly gentleman that had been the source of their cabin ownership. He was being attended to by the family doctor who noted their entrance and his expression was one of deep concern. He stepped out of the room since there was nothing else for him to do for his patient.

At the sight of the foursome, Grandfather rose up a little in bed and managed a smile. He bade them to come closer in almost a whisper. He said, "I don't have much time. My enemies were lucky and found where I have been hiding. One of their minions and I had quite a tussle before he produced the knife that, according to the good doctor here, pierced my liver."

"Hello, Tess, I am so happy to actually meet you though I have been watching you and my young grandson here. I can't tell you how proud I am of you both with your progress in solving my little clues. Perhaps they have been a little overly dramatic, however, as you can see, I have evil and cunning adversaries. I wanted to ensure that Daniel could reap the benefits of my sordid life. My legacy has only been a quest for riches and now that I have had them, I recognize that my family should have been a greater priority. I turned my back when Daniel's father needed me, but I was so fearful that he could be a target. It was not just my riches that my enemies coveted. I had been the source of testimony that put their patriarch behind bars. They are a pack of jackals of which two of their dumbest with whom you have already locked horns."

"Please tell me, did you notice the tobacco tin in the creek and unlock its meaning?"

"Yes, sir. We followed your directions and return to uncover the mine and its shafts. We found the appearance of a gold vein and here is a sample we pulled out of the wall." Daniel responded.

Grandfather forced a smile, "You may have noticed my reference to Shakespeare in my last clue. I have always been a fan of the great Baird so please let me give you the same advice that Polonius gave his son Laertes. 'Beware of entrance to a quarrel, but being in, bear it that the opposed may beware of thee.' You have already caught the attention of my enemies. They probably haven't connected all the dots yet but are trying to determine if you are involved in some way with me. It won't take them too long to figure out our relationship and, the fact that I am alive and in Trail at the same time as you, will verify in their minds that you too should be a target. Beware, but make sure you are prepared for conflict at any time. They are led by the eldest brother of five who took over when his father went to prison. He is cunning and ruthless so be forewarned."

"Hello, my old friend Gus, will you grant me one last promise? Please use your experience and knowledge of the 'bad actors' we have faced together in the past to protect my grandson and your daughter. They don't know what darkness clouds the conscious of those that feel maligned nor the covetousness of the disenfranchised."

"Daniel, I wish our history could have been more traditional, but my life of adventure and misguided values collided with your father and probably would have with you. Your family gave you much more than anything that I could have. You have grown into a fine man of great character, but just remember you have little experience with men that have no integrity. I beg you to be cautious."

With those last words, Grandfather exhaled his last breath.

Tears fell from all four and the doctor once again entered the room. He nodded to Elizabeth, checked his pulse and covered the body of Grandfather. Elizabeth asked the doctor to meet with her in the hallway. As Gus, Tess and Daniel consoled one another and discussed Grandfather's warnings, Elizabeth asked the doctor if he could arrange for the body to be taken to the morgue quietly and a cremation conducted as soon as possible. She understood that this was a murder and would come under the auspices of the Mounties. It would be better, she explained, if Gus, Daniel and Tess were not involved in any investigation since it would likely make them a target just as his patient had been. The doctor had known Elizabeth his entire career and, while concerned about the legal aspects of her request, he assured her that they would not be included in his official report nor in discussions with the authorities.

When Elizabeth rejoined the group, they asked her to explain what had happened. She told them that about two hours ago, she heard a knock at her door. When she opened the door, she was shocked to see grandfather and blood pouring from his jacket. He said that he had been in a fight, was stabbed and turned the knife on his attacker. He didn't know if his assailant had succumbed to his wounds, but was sure he hadn't been followed to her home. He pleaded her not to call a doctor because it would just complicate things. She did not know the extent of his injuries so after she helped him to bed, she ignored his request and called her doctor. She knew the injury was bad, particularly for someone of grandfather's age, but her instincts were to seek professional help. She told them through sobs, that she believed his disappearance long ago had meant that he was dead. She was happy to see him once again, even under these circumstances, and that he could rest in peace having seen his grandson. She was glad that he didn't die alone in some back alley but among people he knew and loved.

The next morning a pair of Mounties arrived at Elizabeth's front door. They asked her to recount the events of the prior evening. They were particularly interested in why Mr. Jacob Johns chose her house to seek refuge. She explained that possibly he knew the address since he had recently sold a cabin to her grand nephew who lives with her. Evidently the good doctor had failed to include Tess, Gus and Daniel in his narrative to the authorities. As she was continuing her dialogue, Bigsby received a call on his two-way radio.

"Well Ma'am I don't think we need to go further. We just received notice that another body was found downstream with stab wounds. Apparently, there was no winner in this battle. We need to go down to secure the body and see if there are any clues. Your home is only a block from the river so we will backtrack and see if we can find the source of the altercation. Thank you for your time. We will be back if we need to shore up any missing pieces."

The Mounties left and Bigsby started to work back to the river while his superintendent drove down to Montrose where the body had drifted. Bigsby could not find any blood trail nor signs of a struggle. After a while, he got a call from Felps who suggested he forgo his search and head to an address that Felps found in the wallet of the deceased.

Bigsby reached the address before Felps and knocked on the front door of the shabby shack. No one answered the knock but Bigsby thought he heard some shuffling inside the crummy looking tenement. When he peeked into a window he saw a scruffy looking hombre heading for the backdoor. The Mountie was waiting for him when he blasted through the door and was quickly subdued by the powerful law man. When Bigsby handcuffed the man, he noticed blood on his shirt. Then he recognized his prisoner as one of the guys he had found following Daniel a few weeks ago. Just then, Felps arrived and walked through the shack before assisting in questioning of the man whom Daniel had labeled as Frack. Frack told the Mounties that he and his brother had been attacked by a 'crazy old man' and his brother had been stabbed. When asked where his brother was now, Frack initially said that he didn't know….that both his brother and the attacker had run off.

"So why would an old man attack two men? What motive could he possibly have?"

"He was crazy, I tell you. We were just walking around and out he came with this large hunting knife." stated Frack.

Was it a knife that looks like this one I just found in your house?" questioned Felps. "And I would like to know, if you weren't cut, why do you have so much blood on your shirt?"

"I, aaaa, tried to help stop the bleeding of my brother."

"I thought you said your brother ran off and you don't know where he is?"

"Did I say that, oh. I tried to help but was afraid the old man might return for me so I ran home. I knew my brother wasn't going to make it so I figured I better get out of there."

"Then maybe you can explain how your brother's body ended up downstream near Montrose?"

"OK, ok, so I figured I could be in trouble, so I dragged him to the river and said goodbye. I was scared and wasn't thinking right."

"Well, it seems you are in possession of the possible murder weapon. We will get a lab test for the blood on your shirt, but I bet it is your brother's and his alone. This sounds pretty bad for you so I suggest you make no further comments until you can see an attorney." Felps said. "Bigsby, please take this person to jail and contact the District Attorney's office."

"But I didn't do anything to my brother!" pleaded Frack.

"That will be for a jury to decide."

The following week Tess, Daniel, Gus and Elizabeth tried to keep low profiles. Grandfather had been cremated and Elizabeth took official control of the urn. Gus drove over to Calgary to have the gold chip assayed. Daniel called his parents and explained that he had met his grandfather, but he had passed soon thereafter. He did not mention the circumstances of his passing nor the gold mine. He had been cautioned by Grandfather of the ruthlessness of his enemies and he wanted to ensure that his parents and sister were as isolated as possible. His parents asked if he could come back to Kaak. They missed him and perhaps he could bring the ashes and fill them in on his life. He agreed that he would love to see them but could only spend the weekend due to his position at the bank. He also asked if Tess and her parents might join him. Certainly they were welcome. They could stay at Sarah's house since she and her husband were traveling that weekend.

While Daniel was anxious to get back to the mine on the weekend, he was excited to see his parents and have them meet Tess. It had been a confusing and exhausting couple of weeks, and he longed for some of the comforts of home. The shock of having met his grandfather and the dire warnings he gave Daniel were an emotional roller-coaster. He almost wished that the gold, the mine and riches hadn't been 'bestowed' upon him. Things were going so well at the bank that he didn't need to have the promises of his grandfather's wealth with the fears that accompanied it. He vowed that he would not follow in his grandfather's footsteps where wealth was the most important thing in his life. He had a growing career, had made some good friends, he loved Trail, his great aunt Elizabeth and the Truesdales were wonderful advocates, he had found someone with whom he wanted to spend his life, and he loved and appreciated his Kaak family. He didn't want to die as his grandfather did nor did he want to see anyone he loved harmed in the quest for yellow money. He decided he would not go back to the mine again. There was just too much risk and he recognized that his priorities should be more noble than digging in the dirt.

When Gus returned with the news that the ore was, indeed, gold bearing, he was surprised when Daniel told him that it didn't matter anymore, he wasn't going to pursue the mine. He explained that he had spoken with Tess on the matter and she had agreed. He didn't want anything that could create danger for her, her family or Daniel's family. Gus reluctantly agreed but suggested that even if they are not involved in the mine's production, the enemies of Grandfather probably wouldn't care. They just wanted the gold for themselves and Daniel or anyone with knowledge of the location of the mine would be a target.

Preparations were made for the weekend trip to Kaak. On Friday afternoon, Tess rode with Daniel driving Elizabeth's jeep and Gus and his wife in their car. Tess and Daniel discussed their future on the drive over. He expressed his desire to spend his life with her and she felt the same way. Daniel feared her leaving for college but, at the same time, didn't want to prohibit her from reaching her dreams. She sensed his concerns and professed that he had become the central item in her life and her future. She was proud of his accomplishments at the bank and felt that they could create a family of their own in Trail. As Daniel had come to the realization that his priorities in life should not be centered on wealth, she felt the same about her college.

The weekend at Daniel's parents went very well. He was doted upon by his parents and, it became obvious, they really liked Tess. Both sets of parents enjoyed long conversations and wonderful home cooked meals. Certainly, there was a bit of a pall over the discussions regarding Grandfather and Daniel made sure that there was no mention of gold, a mine or the fact that grandfather had been intentionally murdered by his enemies. Daniel did hint that grandfather had only wished to protect his family and that was the reason for not financially supporting his son during the hospital stay. Daniel explained that grandfather did have some former acquaintances that might make trouble for his family. On his deathbed, he professed that he wished things could have been different in his relationship with his family. No further mention of the episode was conducted.

As Daniel's mother and Gus's wife were engulfed in conversation, they uncovered a connection that neither had previously known. Daniel's mother was a natural beauty with her high cheekbones and olive skin. Gus's wife, on the other hand was blond, fair and quite tall. To look at the two you would think that neither had any possible blood connections. However, the two ladies discovered that their family trees grew somewhat together through a relationship within the Blackfoot tribe. Daniel's mother was purebred Blackfoot and daughter of the chieftain and had married a white trapper and sired Daniel and Sarah. Her great-grandmother was married to a brave by the name of Climbing Wolf.

"Are you sure of that name? exclaimed Gus's wife. "My mother spoke of her grandfather who had a brother by the Indian name of Climbing Wolf. It is a unique name and I can only wonder if we aren't some distant cousins."

"That could possibly be but why don't we try to make sure and find time to go to the reservation and discuss this with the current chief, your father. He has a vast knowledge of the history of the tribe and would know in an instant how Climbing Wolf's progeny ended up." Responded Daniel's mother. "This is certainly an exciting development!"

Both ladies decided to visit the reservation that fall and see if there was any validity to their hopes.

As the weekend was ending, Daniel's father took him aside for a man-to-man discussion about his intentions with Tess. He was proud of his son's accomplishments and the praise that Gus had confided in him regarding Daniel's career trajectory.

"Son, you've only been gone a few months and your life has changed in so many ways. Your mother and I are so pleased that you seem happy and are both impressed with Tess, her maturity and her devotion to family. It seems to us that she is a 'keeper' and, as you know, I was familiar with Gus and his relationship with my father and there is no finer man. He would have made a fine daughter as well."

"What I'm trying to say is, 'Don't move too fast with your intentions with Tess, but don't let her get away either. Going to college has a way of causing priorities to change. From what we have discussed, your priorities are sound. You want to continue your growing career in Trail and you have a strong urge to settle down with this special young lady. I can't blame you but just be careful. She is a strong woman and you wouldn't want to try and restrict her from fulfilling her destiny. If she truly wants college and career, to stand in her way would be a disaster. On the other hand, if she loves you as much as it appears that you love her, give her reasons to choose to stay with you."

"Thanks, Dad. We've always spoken father to son in the past. I appreciate your advice now as if between two adults. I've grown up a lot in the past few months on my own but will always treasure your advice. Mr. Truesdale once complimented me and said that I must have been brought up right. I have you and Mother to thank for that!"

It was a beautiful day when Sunday arrived, and the foursome headed back to Trail. Tess and her mother decided that they would like to take the Jeep and put the top down to enjoy the ride in the sunshine. While Daniel was unhappy with not being with Tess on the trip back, he harkened his father's words about independent women. Besides, with the trips to the mine no longer an urgency, he could spend more time in Trail with Tess.

On the trip back, Gus and Daniel discussed the episode regarding grandfather and his enemies.

"I can't caution you enough, Daniel, about the type of people grandfather might have made enemies with. He was a tough and shrewd old bird and anyone that earned his fear must surely be formidable. I want you to take special care and watch out for strangers. You have already encountered the two toughs that grandfather had said were the stupid ones. We need to be mindful of the remaining brothers that will surely be seeking vengeance. And they will be just as tough but smarter."

The road between Kaak and Trail was circuitous and, in some places, quite steep. It was a magnificent late summer morning and there was almost no traffic as the two cars drove northward. All of a sudden and inexplicably, the jeep sharply veered off the roadway to the right. Unfortunately, the swerve occurred at a point where the road crested a ravine and the jeep crashed downward. Gus and Daniel were stunned witness to the whole accident and were terrified to see the Jeep disappear. They slammed on brakes and leaped out of their car to rush to the point at which the Jeep crashed. They quickly worked their way downward to where the Jeep lay upright but smashed into a tree. As they reached the accident site, both Tess and her mother were unconscious and bleeding from various cuts on their heads and arms. Gus checked their pulses and both were alive but in pretty bad shape. Gus picked up his wife and told Daniel to carry Tess up the hill to the roadway where they might get some help. Daniel could feel his normally strong legs quiver from fright as he made his way up the hillside. Gus had already placed his wife on a blanket that they had in the car so Daniel laid Tess beside her. Gus shouted for Daniel to take the car to the nearest house for help and he would try to stop the bleeding of his wife who seemed to have the worst damage.

Daniel had noticed a house about a mile back and, rather than hope there was one nearer ahead, he took the prudent course toward Kaak. He stopped at the house and knocked on the door. While people around those parts generally were distrustful of strangers, the man that answered the door immediately took stock of the situation and asked Daniel in. Daniel was covered in his love's blood and the look on his face was proof enough that there had been some form of accident and his guest needed assistance.

"You look like you need help, what happened?"

Daniel explained quickly the details and asked if the man could call an ambulance. The man said he would and would join them with bandages and medicine. At that, Daniel rushed back to the accident only to see Gus in tears leaning over Tess.

"My wife is gone, and my baby is hurt badly." He choked through his sobs.

Daniel could feel his legs momentarily give way as Gus's anguish led to his own terror of what was happening to Tess. For a moment, his shock at the situation caused him to freeze but the arrival of the man from the house brought him back to reality.

"Oh, my God!" exclaimed the man when he saw the two women laying on the blanket. "What can I do to help?"

"There is nothing that can help my poor wife, but we need to stop the bleeding from my daughter's arms. I think she cut an artery and I can't get the bleeding under control."

Daniel and the man took bandages and alcohol to put on Tess's wounds and she had awakened from her coma and was moaning in pain. Each whimper caused Daniel's heart to stop as he tried to be calm under the terrible crisis. They had to stop the bleeding, or she would join her mother. Between the three of them they were able to put bandages and apply pressure to the multiple areas of her arms to stop the flow of blood. Fortunately, an ambulance arrived shortly and took the two ladies to the hospital in Trail. Daniel and Gus thanked the man who said he would look after the Jeep and drove behind the ambulance. They did not speak during the ride as each were absorbed in their own thoughts and fears.

Chapter 9

His mother gave him the Christian name of Matthew in the hopes that he would grow up unlike his father. Matthew's father would eventually sire five evil little misanthropes of which Matthew became the most devious and corrupt. No one ever called him Matthew, nor did many try to call him by name at all. He was generally referred to simply as Stone. Perhaps the moniker became his because of his stoic demeanor, possibly it was because he was tough as a stone, or more likely, it was because he had become a stone-cold killer. More than one unfortunate had passed as a result of his knife, bullets or blows. He was a one-man crime syndicate but had to tolerate his four nitwit brothers. Ever since his father's incarceration, Stone was unfortunately looked upon to reluctantly to lead the misfit crew of his siblings. Now one of them was dead and he had only assigned him to simply monitor what was going on in Trail and to lookout for the old man responsible for his father being in prison.

As Stone sat on in the back seat of his car on the trip from Calgary to Trail, all he could focus upon was his one murdered brother and one of his other younger siblings who was arrested for the killing. His other two brothers were in the front seat with their normal idiotic banter about who was the toughest and why their brothers had been sent to Trail instead of them. He was surprised that he actually felt some remorse over his brothers' disaster in Trail. How could an old man best his two brothers, one by death and the other by guile? Surely, they were a couple of weak-minded oafs, but they were both strong and half the age of their quarry. He pondered the resolve, strength and experience of his rival. He vowed not to underestimate the old man but was equally obsessed with the golden ore that should be his. His father had told him from his prison cell that he had been in a partnership with an older gent from Trail who went simply by the name of J.J. The partners disagreed on the split and his father had taken some of the initial gold findings and fled to Calgary. Unfortunately, the old man had documents and personal connections within the Alberta legal community and Stone's father had to take the fall.

Times had become tough for Matthew's family back in Calgary. The patriarch had been incarcerated, the law was onto his criminal activities and the tax authorities were looking at the family books. In desperation, Stone was conducting this little venture to Trail partly for revenge but also due to a strong need for any capital that might be extracted from the old man. Bile rose in the throat of Stone when he thought of having to flee his hometown under such circumstances. There is little disagreement that the combination of a desperate man, with the touch of

DNA evil that Stone possessed, would not make for anything but a catastrophic outcome.

The only information that Stone possessed regarding the recent activities in Trail was that a young man had moved into the little cottage that belonged to an elderly lady named Elizabeth. This Elizabeth had been around a long time in the city and had once been a credible business lady. She was also purported to be a relative of J.J. She was the only link and Stone decided he would have to make a visit to this Elizabeth and see what information she would provide…..either willingly or under duress. Stone knew just how much pressure would be necessary to know everything he needed.

Unlike his brothers, who wanted to burst into town and start roughing up the old lady, Stone was content to take his time and get to know what he would be up against. He was cunning and would not risk running up against unknown forces. As anxious as he was to get his revenge and his legacy gold, he was disciplined enough to avoid making the same mistakes as his idiot siblings. He would watch and wait, and at the right moment, he would strike. If bodies were left in Trail, so be it, he would have both his revenge and the money that would allow his return to Alberta.

Upon awakening in the hospital, Tess was immediately concerned over the plight of her mother. Both Gus and Daniel had been by her side for the past five hours as she was fighting for her life. She had lost a lot of blood but was spared any trauma to either organs or bones. Tess had been lucky while her mother had not. The look on her father's face when she asked of her mother, told her of the horrible news. Gus was in the pain of grief over his loss, but with Tess's awakening, Gus's heart likewise was awakening to the fact that his daughter was going to live. Tess could feel the tears of both anguish and hope falling on her from her father eyes as he bent over her.

Daniel's brain and soul were in turmoil. Two people that he barely knew were both dead within the same week and his love was nearly torn from him. He was blaming himself for having been the harbinger of bad fate. Had he continued his journey to Vancouver, his grandfather might still be alive and certainly Tess and her mother would not have had the accident. At that instant Tess called out for him and his heart leapt. Careful not to touch her lacerated arms he gently cupped her face in his hands and kissed her on her forehead. All three were crying when the doctor came in to check on his patient and inform them that the x-rays had turned up no major problems except she suffered from some kidney damage. He wanted her to remain in the hospital for a several days for observation due to the psychological impact of her mother's passing and the physical trauma to her body. The doctor administered a sedative and Tess was asleep within minutes.

Gus told Daniel to go back home. He explained that he didn't want to return to the empty house so he would stay at the hospital just to make sure Tess would have him there when she awoke. Daniel was hesitant to leave but was sensitive to Gus's feelings and his obvious remorse over his wife's passing. Daniel called Mr. Truesdale and explained the dreadful news and asked if he could pick him up at the hospital. Mr. Truesdale arrived within a few minutes and the two had a quiet ride back to Daniel's home. As Daniel thanked Mr. Truesdale for the ride, Mr. Truesdale said, "Daniel, you have been through a lot, why not take a couple of days off from the bank and help tend to Gus and Tess. They will certainly need your assistance to deal with the funeral and hospital issues."

"I can't thank you enough for all you have done. I will take you up on your kind offer but will be prepared to get back to work first thing on Wednesday morning." responded Daniel. Before he headed to the cottage, he rang the doorbell at Elizabeth's home. Elizabeth answered the door and could see the anguish on Daniel's face and exclaimed, "Daniel, what has happened? You look distraught!".

Daniel explained the tragedy of the day and apologized for waking her but wanted her to hear the bad news from him first. She thanked him and asked if she could do anything for either Tess or her father.

"I really don't know how Gus will react in the morning when the reality of his loss sets in. I am sure that a visit from you at the hospital would be much appreciated."

With that Daniel went around the house to his cottage in the yard, climbed into bed and was asleep as soon as his head touched the pillow.

The following morning Daniel and Aunt Elizabeth drove to the hospital and took the lift to the recovery room floor. Sitting on a couch was a grim looking Gus who explained that Tess had a bad night with considerable blood in her urine. The pain medications had worn off and the emotional implications of the accident set in. She was asleep now but only because a doctor, making early rounds, gave her some medications to ease the pain. While Elizabeth talked with Gus, Daniel checked in on Tess. She looked distressed even in sleep, as her subconscious was clearly troubled. Daniel stared at the bandaged arms, bruises on her face that now burned a bright yellow and the intravenous fluids entering her scared arm to replace the blood she was losing from her kidneys. Despite the physical

changes, she still looked beautiful to Daniel. He
vowed, that if she survived and would have him, that
he would marry her as soon as she felt up to it. At
this moment nothing meant as much to him as her
recovery. The gold, his career, even his family were
of little consequence as compared with his desire to
live his life with his beautiful companion.

His musings were shattered by the emergency
buzzing sound from one of Tess's monitors.
Immediately, a nurse entered the room and took her
pulse and noted her dropping blood pressure. She
quickly left and within seconds he heard a
loudspeaker request, for the doctor on call, to come
to Tess's room stat. Within minutes the doctor and
two nurses entered the room and Daniel was asked
to leave. He joined Gus and Elizabeth in the waiting
room and explained what had happened. All were
concerned and anxious for the next ten minutes until
the doctor came out and announced that Tess was
stabilized but might need surgery in a few days. He
expressed some trepidation regarding the damage to
her kidneys but wanted to see if the bleeding would
abate on its on or if exploratory surgery might be
necessary. The doctor explained that Tess would
have to be moved to a larger city for an experienced
specialist to perform the surgery. Gus was quick to
say he wanted the very best for his daughter and
would do whatever would be necessary and that cost
would bc no barrier. The doctor simply replied that

all should take a 'wait and see' attitude before making any rash decisions.

Daniel implored Gus to go home and relax a little. A good bath and change of clothes would go far to improve his outlook. The blood of his deceased wife was all over his shirt and was visibly upsetting other visitors to the hospital. Gus agreed and left with Elizabeth, leaving Daniel in the waiting room. The emotions of the past couple of days became too much for Daniel and he simply sat down and cried. In an instant, his life had changed but his strength of conviction remained solid. He would marry Tess if she will still have him.

Stone followed Elizabeth and Gus to the funeral home. He watched as they went into the establishment with their saddened faces and dour demeanor. His initial thought was that Gus was his father's old nemesis and the source of his brother's death. He knew that Elizabeth was the key and here she was with a man that was about the right age and someone that would make a physically formidable foe. If he was, indeed, the killer of his little brother, Stone could now understand how that might have occurred. This man looked powerful and had a presence that would cause men to be wary about crossing him. Stone, of course, merely observed him as the mongoose views his cobra: A dangerous adversary but aware that the odds would be in his favor.

When the couple left the mortuary, Stone entered the establishment and inquired about upcoming funerals. The mortician told him that the gentleman who just left had lost his wife to an automobile accident and the services would be tomorrow. This came as a surprise to Stone because he was pretty sure his father's partner had been a long-term widower. He retreated from the funeral parlor and headed back to the apartment the siblings had rented for the month. There he instructed one of his brothers to monitor the comings and goings at Elizabeth's home. Eventually, this J.J. character would appear but if he didn't, Stone would seek a more direct method of finding his nemesis. He had no doubts that a few minutes of 'interrogation' with Lady Elizabeth would prove informative.

Tess was unable to attend the cremation of her mother, so a memorial would be established sometime in the future. Daniel had called his parents with the terrible news and they expressed their shock and offered anything they could do for poor Tess or her father. In front of Daniel, Tess tried to present a brave front, but it was obvious she was in deep despair. As soon as her father would enter the room she would burst out in tears and anguish for both of their losses. It was breaking Daniel's heart as the tears flowed from the two people he had come to love deeply.

Daniel didn't wish to leave Mr. Truesdale without his senior lending officer so he worked every day but visited the improving Tess every lunch hour and every evening. She was getting stronger and receiving favorable reports from the doctors who were monitoring her. The progress of her healing lacerations was promising, however, one of her kidneys required several surgical procedures. Unfortunately, the doctors felt that she would need a more radical kidney repair in a major hospital that supported a kidney specialist. The hospital bills were becoming enormous and, despite Gus's reasonable financial position, Daniel could tell that he was worried. The cost of the jeep, the funeral, the hospital and doctors' bills were starting to wear on the man. And his daughter would need to go to Vancouver for the advanced procedure.

When she was well enough to travel, Gus rode in the ambulance with Tess to St. Paul's Hospital in downtown Vancouver. The hospital had a wonderful reputation, having been run by a Catholic order since the late 1800's. She would have extensive care there and, despite Daniel's feeling of abandonment, he knew this was for the best. He called her every evening from Elizabeth's phone. On the day of the surgery, he asked Mr. Truesdale if he could take two days off and borrowed Elizabeth's new jeep for the trek to Vancouver. He had the mixed emotions of fear for the surgery's outcome but excitement to see the city that had once, not too long ago, been his life's goal. Now, as fate had dipped into his soul, he knew in his heart, that his destiny was not in the big city. Still, he felt a tingle of interest in what he would be missing.

Tess's surgery went well and the doctors were pleased with her body's reaction to the procedure. They felt that she would be cleared to travel back to Trail in three or four days if she didn't develop any infection or other surgery-related maladies. She was happy to return home, as was Daniel when she told him the news. She knew he had to return on the six-hundred-kilometer drive and begged him to be careful. Gus informed him that they would return as soon as possible but would take an ambulance for the ride home as an extra precaution.

With the disappearance of Gus and the lack of anyone that matched the appearance of his quarry, Stone was growing weary of watching Elizabeth. He needed an infusion of money and she was the only link that he had in finding his father's mine. In desperation, he decided to pay Elizabeth a visit. He watched her house to make sure there was no one visiting and knocked on her door. As she opened the door, he forced his way in only to be whacked on the knee by Elizabeth's cane. He groaned but regained his strength enough to push her to the floor and sit on top of her waist. His weight made her struggle to breathe and he held his knife at her temple.

"Where is my father's mine? I know you and your old relative J.J. are tight and he has probably told you just where it is. I need to know, and I need it right now. Tell me and you live, don't and I will torture you until he shows up!"

"My brother-in-law is dead and with him died any knowledge of a mine yours or his." She was able to whisper out under the weight of the intruder.

At that moment Daniel drove in from Vancouver and was going to return the jeep when he noticed the front door was open. He called out, "Aunt Elizabeth, is everything alright?" Having heard nothing, he jumped up the steps to the porch and entered the dark foyer. Immediately, he felt the back of his head being smashed and he crashed to the ground. The last thing he heard before he blacked out was the shrill whistle that all Mounties carry.

Sargent Bigsby had been making his rounds when he saw Daniel enter Elizabeth's home. When he heard a muffled cry and a crash, he blew his whistle and ascended the steps. Through the dim light he saw two prone figures and could hear footsteps as Stone ran through the house and out the back door. Bigsby stopped when he noticed the female figure on the floor was gasping and he turned on a light. There he saw the unconscious Daniel with blood on his scalp and Elizabeth who was trying to catch her breath. He propped up Elizabeth who pointed at her nephew who was starting to come to.

Bigsby enquired, "What just happened, and did I hear someone leaving through the back door?"

"There was a man who knocked on the door and pushed his way in. I don't know if he intended to rob me or if he had some sort of vendetta against me. He was strong and when my nephew came to check on me, the villain hit him when he entered the threshold."

About that time Daniel began to stir and questioned what was going on. For a minute he thought that Bigsby was involved in the assault. "What are you doing to my aunt?" he exclaimed while clenching his fists ready for a fight.

"No, Daniel, it wasn't the Sargent. He is the reason we are safe now. There was an intruder that had me powerless until you came along, then he turned his attentions to you and that's how you have that knot that is starting to form on your head. We need to get you some ice and get you into my parlor."

Bigsby set about gathering any evidence that might lead to the identity of the intruder. He checked for footprints in both the front and back yards and in the back yard he found a pair of cheap gloves thrown into the hedge. In his mind, that probably meant that tomorrow when they dust the front door for prints, there will likely be none. Likewise, he found no heel to toe prints anywhere on the ground other than those that matched Daniel's boots. Instead he did see some toe to arch prints, somewhat reminiscent of the stealthy movement of Indians. Whoever this was, he was a cautious individual. The real question in Bigsby's mind was why?

Daniel was making a bit of a recovery with the cold pack and starting to understand the implications of the attack on Elizabeth. Evidently, someone associated with Frick and Frack was looking for information regarding his grandfather. Clearly grandfather's enemies had put two and two together and decided that they would try and extract information in an aggressive fashion. Anger rose in Daniel as he thought of some ruffian treating his great aunt with such physical means. Still a bit groggy, he attempted to stand and chase after the intruder only to collapse back on the floor. He was not in any shape yet to seek retribution, but that frustration only added to Daniel's fury. That rage would have to wait until tomorrow.

Sargent Bigsby and Elizabeth assisted Daniel to his cottage with strict orders for him to get some rest. The ordeal with Gus's wife, Tess's medical condition and now his injury and concern for Elizabeth had taken a toll of Daniel's mental and physical situation. Bigsby assured Daniel that he would remain on guard on the premises just in case the perpetrator decided to return. Daniel was grateful and as he was thanking the Mountie, he fell into a deep sleep.

When the sun arose, so did Daniel and he was up and ready to catch up with Bigsby. He found the Sargent on Elizabeth's front porch discussing the situation with Superintendent Felps. As he approached them he overheard their discussions.

 "I can only think that there is some link to the death of the elderly gentleman and this recent attack. Two issues on this very threshold, within days, in our little town is just too coincidental. Maybe you were right that there is some connection between the young banker, the dead man and Miss Elizabeth," expressed Felps.

"I just have a better feeling about young Daniel than I once had," said Bigsby. "He seems pretty much a straight up guy. His coworkers seem to like him, certainly Mr. Truesdale is smitten with him, and he seems to avoid trouble though it may be following him. I say we spend our time looking for this new element in our fine town and see if we can 'encourage' him to leave. There can't be too many places that a newcomer can be staying so let's take a look around town."

It was a great idea from the Mountie perspective, but Matthew was well aware of the dangers of keeping a presence in such a small town as Trail. His presence and even the license plates on his car would stir up conversation in such an insular place. He was too crafty for that, so he abandoned the rental house and had one of his brothers call about renting a cabin up in the mountains far enough away from Trail to be isolated but close enough to make visits to gain information. The cabin was owned by a hunting associate in Alberta so there would be no paper trail and far enough off paved roads to hide their vehicle.

After last night's episode, Matthew vowed to only enter the town in the darkness and with extreme caution. He MUST find a way to kidnap that Elizabeth lady, bring her to the safety of his cabin and use whatever means to interrogate her. He must have the treasure that his father had left behind. He couldn't risk any attempt to grab her at her house. That pesky kid and now the Mounties will be overly cautious and likely to install alarm systems or step up patrols in the vicinity. He would have to send one of his brothers to monitor if she has any particular life patterns- when she goes grocery shopping, when she plays cards, when she goes to church. If she has a routine, and Matthew knew that most people do, they could make plans for a snatch that would be away from alarms and legal interlopers.

When Daniel made his presence known, the Mounties went silent.

"What have you learned so far?" he inquired.

"Just as we expected, there were no prints on the door handle or on the frame of the back door, which, by the way, he smashed on his way out. No discernable shoe markings but we know from the width of the sole that he is quite heavy and pretty large. Do you recall any features of the man?"

I am afraid not, I just focused on Aunt Elizabeth and was hit from behind, so I only saw what seemed like shadows," responded Daniel. "I think it would be wise to have my aunt leave town until you fellows can catch this dangerous man. In fact, I am on my way in to call my mother and see about Elizabeth visiting her for a while."

"That may be a good idea, but we think there is some connection between the death of that man on her porch and why she was attacked last night. In any regard, we would like her to be available in case we can determine whatever that connection might entail."

"Well, I can appreciate that, but you must realize that the safety of my aunt comes first and unless you wish to arrest her, I would feel much better if she was out of town for a while. I trust you will be able to 'get your man'. Isn't that what the Mounties always say? I am sorry if I appear rude, my only concern is to get her away from any danger that may still be lurking around Trail. I will promise that she can be available to answer any of your questions by phone or if you catch the perpetrator she will return."

"That seems reasonable." The two law men agreed. "And since 'we always get our man' her vacation may be short-lived." They laughed.

The Mounties were still chuckling when a wrecker truck carrying the remains of Elizbeth's jeep drove up. A man got out of the truck and asked if this was the correct address of the owner. He also said, "I'm glad to run into you Mounties because this seems to have been no accident."

"How so?" responded Superintendent Felps.

"Well it appears that the right tie rod was deliberately sawed, leaving only a small area to support any right turn. The switchbacks where we found the vehicle could have placed enough tension on the rocker and tie rod that snapped, causing the jeep to veer to the right. That explains why the vehicle made a sudden turn down the mountainside."

Felps asked the mechanic to take the jeep to the impound lot at the Mounties' station for evidence of a crime. "Now we have a manslaughter on our hands, Daniel, and you and your aunt have some explaining to do! Please come down to headquarters when she feels up to answering some questions."

"We certainly will," Daniel said, just barely keeping his anger under control. Someone was trying to kill either he or Elizabeth and, unfortunately, it was Tess and her mother that bore the brunt of the plot.

Daniel told Elizabeth about the situation regarding the jeep and the attempt to make the crash look like an accident. He asked her if she felt up to going to the Mounties and making a statement. They both felt that things had gotten out of control and that they would tell the Mounties about everything except the mine. Daniel asked Elizabeth if she felt ok about staying with his parents back in Kaak. Under the circumstances, her life was certainly in danger and Daniel had to look after Tess. She agreed and together they called Daniel's mother.

On the call, Daniel explained what had happened and suggested that Elizabeth would be safer if she could visit them. Daniel's mother said however, "I may have a better idea. I wrote my father and Tess' great uncle on the Reservation about visiting them. I was planning on including Tess' mother and we were going to research our relationship with Climbing Wolf. I could drive over to Trail and pick up Elizabeth and we could both go to the Reservation. We would be safe there and it would be closer to Trail. I want you to be careful too. We don't know who are these people, and they are certainly willing to kill to get what they want."

Daniel's mother said she would start immediately since she was already packed, would pick up Elizabeth and then head over to the Reservation. This idea seemed acceptable to Elizabeth and she went upstairs to pack. As soon as she returned, they drove over to see the Mounties. They explained everything to the Mounties who were not particularly happy about the details regarding Daniel's grandfather but felt that they had enough information to make sense of the two deaths and the attempt on Elizabeth. Daniel explained that his grandfather's enemies believed he had some form of treasure and had been hunting him for several years. Other than that, Daniel had no idea who they were or where any treasure might be. Daniel told them that he felt that it would be safer for Elizabeth to be out of town and away from whomever might be trying to obtain information from her. They agreed and wished her safe journey but to contact them as soon as she returned.

They drove back to Elizabeth's house and waited for Daniel's mother to arrive. She got there late afternoon and, after hugging and warning Daniel, they took off for the Blackfoot Reservation. Unfortunately, one of Stone's brothers had seen the two ladies' departure and decided to follow them. When they got to the Reservation, he stopped, not knowing what to do on Indian land. He returned to the cabin where Stone and his brother were waiting.

"You finally did something right, little brother." Glad you followed them and equally pleased that you didn't intrude on Indian property. They can be downright hostile if they smell something is not right and a white man following two ladies would not sit well. We will pay a visit there but not before I do some recon on the territory. I will call the owner of this cabin and get a feel for the Blackfoot tribe."

Meanwhile, Daniel's mother and aunt got settled into the property's lodge and met with the tribal elder. They explained that they were trying to avoid some bad people and wanted to meet with Daniel's maternal grandfather Chief Climbing Wolf. The elder thought for a few minutes and said he would send for Climbing Wolf who was out on a remote part of the Reservation but suggested that they should also meet an old brave named Lone Wolf. The elder explained that Lone Wolf would be a good bodyguard for them while on the Rez. He didn't expect any trouble, but it couldn't hurt to have a backup.

"Lone Wolf is a born tracker and is extremely loyal. Like the famed Gurkhas who protect the queen and the Swiss Guards who were bodyguards over the French Royalty, Lone Wolf is single-minded in his duty of fidelity. Despite his age he will ensure that you are safe while on Blackfoot territory!"

"You really know your history." pronounced Elizabeth.

"I was educated in Vancouver at the University of British Columbia and really focused on history and have a book published on indigenous people in Canada."

"That is impressive, and we appreciate your hospitality and look forward to meeting both Lone Wolf and seeing my father." Added Daniel's mother.

"Well Lone Wolf is here now so I will send him around to meet with you at the lodge. He is getting on in years but is still quite able and I am sure you will like him. Climbing Wolf is out but is scheduled to return in the next day or so. Please make yourself comfortable and I know that Climbing Wolf will be anxious to see you and hear about his in-law, though departed. It's been a while since you've visited, and we welcome your return.

Elizabeth and Daniel's mother each had rooms in the lodge and were sitting in the great room when Lone Wolf entered and introduced himself. He spoke little English but was quite engaged with the two ladies. It was obvious he was proud to be given the task of ensuring their safety and he was noticeably pleased that he would be spending time with ladies. Like many before him that had been lions in their youth, the sands of time had taken away the esteem that he once held in the tribe. This was a chance at youth revisited and an opportunity to show that he was not an irrelevant encumbrance to the tribe.

The ladies were delighted with their new-found friend and were pleased that the elder had assigned such a perfect person to serve as their guide and guardian. It had been an exhausting day and the two decided to skip dinner and head straight for bed but not before they asked if Lone Wolf could show them around in the morning. He was pleased to take them to the communal breakfast and would walk them around the tribal settlement.

The following week began to show signs of the rapidly approaching autumn. The treetops were starting to turn and there became the familiar crispness to the breeze. Daniel worked as best he could at the bank while worrying about Tess and would call her from Elizabeth's house each evening.

Her voice always tried to be upbeat, however, he could sense that she was putting on a brave front. Gus would tell him that she was improving every day, but the doctors would not release her to come home. That worried Daniel and he prayed each night that she would return and be with him forever. He kept a watchful eye every day and would use the tunnel each evening to wander around the area looking for anyone that might represent a threat. It seems that a calm had started to prevail around the town, and the daily reports from the Mounties were also benign.

Things at Stone's cabin, however, were not so calm. They were busily plotting how to nab Elizabeth and return her to where they could get the answers they needed. They were having a hard time getting any information about the reservation but had found a place just off the Indian territory where they could hide a car. How far they might have to go on foot was completely unknown, but they were becoming desperate. Stone decided that his two brothers would do some reconnaissance hiking on the Rez while Stone stayed in the car. Neither brother relished the task of hiking through the backwoods with the possibility of being treated as a trespasser if caught. Tribal law would prevail, and they had no idea what type of punishment might accompany their transgressions. While they were afraid of running into Indian trouble, they were considerably more afraid of angering their older brother. So, all agreed that the kidnap had to occur early the next morning.

Meanwhile on the reservation, the two ladies had become extremely fond of their guide and guardian. He was respectful but sometimes playful. He was, however, ever vigilant for their safety. It was rugged country and he was impressed with their desire to explore and ability to face craggy terrain. On one morning's mountain hike, however, Daniel's mother slipped and cut her knee on a jagged rock outcropping. While the injury was not serious, Lone Wolf accompanied her back to the lodge. Meanwhile Elizabeth wished to continue up the slope to see the view of the rising sun. While Lone Wolf would have preferred to have Elizabeth return with him, she insisted that she would be fine and would wait for him at the summit.

When he returned, he saw the older lady climbing toward the mountain's peak. She was arduously making her way up the mountainside completely unaware that she was being followed. Lone Wolf knew, however, and was tracking and watching. He had seen the heel-to-toe marks of the boots of two men that should not be here. He knew he was invisible to both the hunters and the hunted. The skill of being unseen had served him well all his life and he had no fear of being seen now. His strength was in concealment and patience. Like his namesake, he was a lone predator, and, in his self-reliance, he knew no fear. He was a survivor and now he was a protector. And he was invisible.

His attention turned to the two men that were following the lady. They stayed a distance from her but slowly climbed side by side. Sometimes they would even talk together. He recognized that they were not good hunters but were still a threat to the lady whose safety had been entrusted to him. After their last conversation, they began to speed up and it was apparent they were closing in on the unsuspecting lady. Each withdrew a hand-gun from their waistbands. Just like his tribe had, for centuries, chased their prey, the two men were moving quickly with the malice of hunters anticipating the kill. It was then that he decided to attack.

The lady turned when she heard Lone Wolf's war cry and subsequent scream of the first man who bore the brunt of the Indian's attack. The hundred and ninety pounds of warrior fury knocked the man on the ground and a rock against the man's temple made a quick death to the hunter. Before the second man could react with his weapon, Lone Wolf turned on him. The man tried to escape but backed into a crevasse and fell to his death.

Elizabeth rapidly made her way down the mountain to where Lone Wolf was checking the two hunters. Both were dead and Lone Wolf had already retrieved their handguns. In an instant Elizabeth recognized a resemblance of the two brothers to the man that had attacked her in Trail. While she was shaken at the thought of the two dead men, she was just as angry that she had been singled out for such a cowardly attack on her person. She hugged Lone Wolf and they set out to return to the lodge and to alert Tribal Counsel. Back at the lodge word spread quickly of the event, and Chief Climbing Wolf immediately called on the two ladies. They explained the circumstances, yet he was concerned over the death of two white men on Blackfoot land. Surely, there would be repercussions and Lone Wolf might have to go to jail. Elizabeth explained about her previous attack in Trail and the resemblance of her attacker to the two dead men. She expressed her sincere belief that, had Lone Wolf not been so resourceful and capable, she would have surely been kidnapped. The Mounties were aware of her enemies and would not have anything but praise for the quick actions of Lone Wolf. With that explanation, the Chief appeared more at ease and requested Lone Wolf to meet with the Tribal Elders.

At the gathering of the Counsel, Elizabeth provided the entire narrative and expressed her admiration for the bravery of the elder warrior to go against two armed young men. She assured the Elders that she would inform the Mounties that Lone Wolf acted in an honorable and prudent fashion given the circumstances, and the only malice involved came from the two-armed white hunters.

With all the excitement and praise from Elizabeth, Lone Wolf was reveling in the attention. He noticed when he walked from the gathering, his tribe looked on him like when he was a young brave. Even the Chief made eye contact with him and gave him a bit of a smile. The old lion still had fangs and Lone Wolf's exploits that day would be talked about for many years to come.

The bodies were recovered, and the Chief made a telephone call to the Mountie office in Trail. After hearing of the story, Superintendent Felps said he would drive out there immediately and initiate his investigation. Since the situation occurred on tribal land, tribal laws would prevail, but he would assist, if requested, and take responsibility of the two deceased. He wondered how his jailed murder suspect would react when he was told of two more fatalities that are most likely kinfolk.

Daniel's mother called her son and told him of the happenings of the morning. He expressed his relief that everything had turned out well but had trepidations that there was at least one of his grandfather's enemies for which was unaccounted. The description of the two men did not match his attacker at Elizabeth's home. He wished to thank the Chief and Lone Wolf for their protection and would meet with Superintendent Felps when he returned to Trail.

Meanwhile, Stone was growing concerned about his brothers and their prolonged incursion into tribal property. Maybe they had found the old lady and were dragging her back to the car. More likely, however, they had been caught and detained. Just as these thoughts were meandering through his mind, the sound of a siren and a cruiser with the Mountie insignia rushed past his concealed car.

Chapter 10

While Tess was delighted to return to Trail from the big city and the hustle and bustle of a major medical facility, the moment she stepped into the house, she burst into tears. The memories of her mother flooded her mind and blocked out any fondness she had for Trail, the mine and even Daniel. Gus was mindful of her condition and suggested that they move into Elizabeth's house until time dulled the knife that was tearing at Tess's heart. She thought that a reasonable course until Daniel arrived and explained the attack at the threshold of Elizabeth's home and the tragedy on the reservation. After some discussion, the three decided that they would go back to the mine and the little cabin and try to 'hide out' from the realities of a parental loss and the aggressive actions of an unknown antagonist. They could build onto the cabin and make it habitable for three people while becoming 'invisible', much the lone wolf of Daniel's long-ago dream.

Daniel was fearful of this last enemy. He had already felt the strength and resolve of the man who hit him in his aunt's foyer. In any wild animal that is either starving, injured or with his back to a wall, their fierceness increases tenfold. His last antagonist was probably suffering from all three. He was clearly hungry for his grandfather's gold, he had been injured by losing his clan and must be feeling trapped and afraid. Certainly, a recipe for danger that caused the hair on the back of Daniel's neck to rise.

Daniel raced back to Elizabeth's house to call Mr. Truesdale and his father and inform them of what had transpired on the reservation. To Mr. Truesdale, he simply asked him if he could take a few days off to tend to Lady Tess. His request was immediately granted and Truesdale asked if he could be of any assistance. Daniel just suggested that he keep a watchful eye for any strangers that might be asking about him or Elizabeth at the bank. To his father, Daniel expressed his concern for Tess, Gus and his family in Kaak.

"After this assault on Mother and Aunt Elizabeth, I don't know what is best. I felt that they would be safe on the reservation but, even there, they were found by Grandfather's enemies."

"Glad you told me, son, and I am so grateful that they were unharmed. I have the Chief's telephone number and will call him immediately. I plan on going up there and bringing them back here where I can keep a watchful eye."

"Please be careful, father, I didn't want any of our family to be involved. I realize that this is the only alternative now, and Gus, Tess and I will be moving to Grandfather's old cabin until this gets resolved. We have been careful to not be followed whenever going there, so it is a safe place. Please tell Sarah what has been going on and beg her to be careful. We just don't know where or when this enemy might show up."

"I know you don't have any way to communicate up on the mountain, so please find a phone and call me every so often. We will be worried about you, but I know you can take care of yourself. I love you and want you to be careful. I am going to call the reservation now. Kiss Tess for me."

Daniel went into his cottage and packed a few essentials and the bear gun that Elizabeth had lent him. Careful to not be spotted, he slid down into his escape tunnel and popped out in the vacant lot and headed to Gus and Tess' house. They were packing the car when he arrived, and he was finally able to hold Tess for the first time in too many days. He kissed her cheek and could taste the tears that ran down from her swollen eyes. He realized that it would take time before she could get over her mother's sudden death, but his concern now was for her safety. He felt guilty that he had been responsible for her mother's death and prayed that Tess would forgive him. They finished the packing and took the car on a circuitous route that ended in the tiny dirt road that was closest to the base of the mountain. Tomorrow, they would clear another spur to the road where they could better hide the car. For the afternoon, however, they needed to climb to the cabin and make it more livable for the three 'campers'.

Tess's mood was gradually improving as the beauty of the surrounding mountains and the clear cool air stimulated her senses. She even gave Daniel a little smile which helped a bit to ease his feeling of guilt.

When they finally reached the cabin, they were exhausted from the climb, the fear, and the emotions of the past few days. Daniel lit the two oil lamps that had been in the cabin and each made a pallet where they could rest. Gus and Tess immediately fell asleep, but Daniel was too much on edge to close his eyes. Instead he was thinking of how they could prepare the cabin for safety and expansion to provide more comfort and privacy. Also, they would need money for supplies and building material, not to mention the massive doctor and hospital bills. He could use the mines' gold to satisfy some of the need for cash, but that would take time and present an element of danger in transporting the gold and converting it into ready cash. As he was pondering all this in his head, he eventually fell into a deep sleep.

When Daniel awoke, he knew the answer to his desperate need for cash. He felt like an enormous burden was lifted off his shoulders and could now focus on expanding the cabin. He started a fire in the fireplace as the early fall shortened days made for a chilly morning. The smell of the burning logs reminded him of his youthful days back in Kaak when his dad made the fire prior to going on his trap lines. As he made coffee for the threesome, Tess awoke and came over to Daniel and delivered such a passionate kiss that he was fearful that Gus would awaken and think poorly of the two. He held her tightly and could feel her curves caressing his whole body. His physical response was obvious, and in their minds, each recalled the lovemaking that had occurred in this very cabin not too long ago. Their musings were abruptly cut short when Gus snorted when smelling the percolating coffee. They immediately parted and Daniel turned away as the manifestation of his desire for Tess was obvious. Gus hacked and snorted and ultimately woke himself. He sat on the end of the bed looking confused at his surroundings until at last said, "I guess this explains why my back is sore, my legs ache and I'm hungrier than a pirate abandoned on Dead Chest Island!"

The comment broke up the twosome as they laughed at Gus's nautical metaphor. Deep in the Canadian Rockies in a tiny log cabin to hear of pirates and islands seemed so out of place. They drank coffee and Daniel explained his thoughts regarding expanding the cabin and his revelation regarding their need for funds. All agreed that the cabin needed to be increased in size, and that expansion should incorporate abutting the tree that permitted entrance into the mine. By having an ability to climb from within the house into the hidden door of the tree, no casual visitor could see their comings and goings. This seemed to make sense to all and they set about drawing the schematic that would incorporate that factor into their renderings. Gus was the natural builder so he laid out the plans for the expansion and a connection to the base of the tree that would look natural. They would need to cut trees but didn't want to 'lose' the visual protection that they provided the cabin. Gus explained that trees needed to be cut above the cabin and dragged down, and someone would need to go into town for construction supplies. They would need a generator for electricity, a pump for bringing running water into the cabin from the well, lights and a heater.

"I have to go into work in a couple of days and I can pick up whatever you need," said Daniel. "If my plan to raise funds is going to work, things need to appear to be as natural as possible."

Tess immediately responded, "I don't think this is a good idea. Can't we find some other way of paying the bills?"

"Honestly, Tess, I don't see any alternative. With the purchase of the tar sands by your dad, his money is tied up for now. We must remain safe and we need to pay all these expenses of modernizing the cabin and your hospital bills. The results of the mine will come too slowly and we need to get moving now. I will be safe at the bank and at Elizabeth's cottage for a few days and will be especially cautious."

"Still, I wish there was a better way," she sighed

The next two days were filled with cutting and sizing logs for the cabin addition. They were able to fell a sufficient number of trees to complete the addition and position them to create the walls. Lumber would have to be purchased for the roof and flooring so several trips would need to be made in order to not draw suspicions. Daniel drove into town six times to obtain what they needed and used what little cash they had to obtain the needed supplies, lumber and equipment.

It was a Wednesday when Daniel entered the bank to resume his duties as the Senior Lending Officer. He was well-greeted by his co-workers and Mr. Truesdale, and spent much of the day working with managers to develop plans and a budget for the coming new year. Daniel worked hard and gained the admiration of his co-workers. Each evening after work he arrived after dark at Elizabeth's little cottage, he would quickly slip in and lock the door and never turn on any lights. If he happened to awaken during night, he would walk around

Elizabeth's house to see if there was any sign of forced entry or anyone watching the house. He was grateful that these scans turned up empty.

On Friday, Mr. Truesdale was out of town and it was Daniel's responsibility to perform the week's final accounting. There was more cash on hand than usual since the smelter's payroll was due out on Monday so auditing would take a bit longer than usual. During the day, Daniel prepared a letter and a document for Mr. Truesdale and left it on his desk. Daniel set the alarm, closed, and locked the bank. He would spend the weekend in his cottage and head for Vancouver on Sunday. With him would be the million dollars that he had taken from the bank.

In the cabin, Gus and Tess tried to stay busy with the construction onto the addition. The sadness of their loss, together with concerns over Daniel, placed a pall over the weekend. They were able to get the logs into place for the walls and set the roof trusses. Gus's enormous strength made up for the still-weakened Tess, but she was gradually improving physically. For Tess, this whole summer has been a whirlwind of emotions. She truly felt that she had met the one person in her life that could make her happy now and forever. Just the thought of him would make her quiver with excitement and smile with satisfaction. It was a pattern of emotions that had no precedence nor any precept of ending. Her mother's abrupt passing, however, led to uncontrollable angst and overwhelming sadness. Her loss was almost unbearable and without any consolation. Only the constant attention by her father kept her from falling into a state of mental oblivion. He forced her into activity on the construction just as much to provide her some mental and physical stimulation as it was to assist him in the effort.

It was a dreary cold morning when Daniel left for Vancouver. The somber weather only added to his feeling of aloneness and foreboding. From listening to stories on his radio years ago, he recalled an artistic and literary portrayal of the Pathetic Fallacy. Certainly, the combination of his melancholy mood fit the gloomy and oppressive sky. He had taken a big chance with the money but couldn't think of any alternative. He hoped Mr. Truesdale would understand and not think that this was his payment for all the kindness and trust he had placed in Daniel's hands. Throughout history the term 'betrayal' invariably described mankind's worst characteristics. Daniel had always considered himself to be an honorable man, a trustworthy man. Certainly, this act would not be perceived as anything but a selfish gesture, something that his grandfather had warned him against. Still, Daniel felt that this was the only alternative and, if all the stars came together, the ending might just justify the extraordinary means.

Stone was holed up in his hunting lodge like a wounded animal. He had lost just about everything and was at the point at which desperation was surmounting reason and caution. The Mounties in Trail were looking for him, the tax authorities in Alberta were hot after him and his criminal empire was, for all intents and purposes, shut down. With his siblings either incarcerated or dead, he had no support and even worse, no one to boss around. Mundane tasks that he normally assigned to his brothers, he had to perform for himself. He didn't like that! Inevitably, predators lick their wounds and return to their carnivorous habits. To survive, they must be faster, fiercer or more cunning than their prey. Stone had figured out that the old lady and her young tenant were somehow connected to his father's old partner. Since the partner seems to have vanished, Stone would take his revenge on the twosome. They were now his prey.

The Monday sun had barely risen in the shortening days of autumn in the Rockies when the Head Cashier unlocked the bank. She noticed a singular letter on Mr. Truesdale's desk but nothing else seemed unusual as she progressed through her morning routine. It wouldn't be until the manager arrived and the two of them opened the vault that anything seemed out of the ordinary. As they rolled out the cash drawers, however, there was nothing in them! Clearly, there was at least a million dollars missing. They conferred and made two telephone calls: first to the Mounties, secondly to Mr. Truesdale. Had the order of calls been reversed, the sequence of subsequent events would have changed drastically. History doesn't always move in the most straightforward progression.

The Mounties arrived almost immediately and began their investigation. They took fingerprints and interviewed the Head Cashier and the Manager. They looked at the alarm system and employee time logs. The glaring issue was the absence of Daniel and the fact that he was the last person in the bank. About that time Mr. Truesdale arrived and held a private conference with the Mounties. As he was listening to the Mounties, he noticed the letter, in Daniel's handwriting, sitting on his desk. He took up the letter, read it and began to smile.

As the Mounties continued their investigation, they decided that they would issue an arrest citation for Daniel. Despite protestations by Mr. Truesdale who insisted that he did not wish to press charges, the Mounties indicated that this was a federal issue and, as such, was outside their control. Authorities across the country would be alerted and a manhunt would be initiated. Bank robbery is an issue that is not taken lightly, they explained, and due process would be conducted.

The owner of the funeral home that took care of Gus' wife awoke to find an envelope that contained exactly the cost of the funeral. He felt it unusual that Gus would have paid the considerable sum in cash but was pleased that the bill was paid and could go into his account that morning. Likewise, the owner of the garage that recovered the jeep, found a similar envelope to cover his cost of the extraction and delivery of the vehicle. Also, the good Samaritan that assisted during the crash discovered a few hundred dollars in his mailbox that morning with no explanation. Just as he had been an unknown responder in time of need, this envelope held no one to thank.

Separately, Sargent Bigsby had questions about this recent turn of events. Something in his mind didn't add up. Despite his earlier concerns and dislike for the foreigner, Bigsby recognized that Daniel seemed an honest young person who had progressed in the bank rapidly. He didn't seem arrogant or manipulative. Bigsby knew of the details of the accident that took Tess's mother and the angst that it caused to the family. Daniel had been there as the support that Gus and Tess needed in this time of sorrow. It didn't make sense to him that Daniel would throw all his future away for the sake of a million dollars. Plus, he seemed to be the prey of some really nefarious outsiders. He hoped he would be able to determine the reason for this total change of character.

Six hundred kilometers to the west Daniel was busy paying off the hospital and the doctors that had administered to Tess during her prolonged stay. It turned out to be a beautiful day in the city with a slightly brisk breeze coming off the sound. As Daniel strolled around the city his mind wandered about what it would have been like to have completed his journey and settled in this glorious metropolis. He was too young to understand the course of life and the decisions that have to be made and the implications of those decisions. At this moment, he felt a little conflicted. His life in Trail had been glorious for a boy from a town as small as Kaak. Now he wondered if that glory could ever be recovered or should he pursue his original dream. He had betrayed his friend and the entire community that had shown him their hospitality. How could he ever recover that misplaced trust? What would his family think when they heard of his deeds? He had thought all this through in his mind but now that he had crossed that Rubicon, he had second thoughts about how it would be perceived. However, his love for Tess was his guiding force and, if he would be castigated for his methods, that would just have to be. In his mind, he was doing the right thing, the honorable thing, and if others judged him otherwise that was beyond his control. All beauty of the city aside, he must return to Tess, to Gus, to Mr. Truesdale and to the man who is likely trying to kill him.

Chapter 11

Daniel knew that his removal of the money from the bank would create quite a firestorm in the legal community. He was, however (and very unfortunately) unaware of the nature of law enforcement when it involves federal banking laws. Before he even left Vancouver, he saw his picture and a description of Gus' car on the billboard of the post office. He had gone there to mail one final bit of cash to a pharmacist from whom Gus had obtained some pain medicine for Tess's trip back to Trail. This was the one last loose end and Daniel dropped the letter from his hand when he saw the Wanted Poster. His hands trembled and sweat poured from his brow as he picked up the letter and placed it in the mail slot.

When he returned to the car, he knew he needed to alter the looks of Gus's vehicle and use some form of disguise if he was to make it back to Trail. Fortunately, he realized that any law enforcement would be looking for him to be fleeing from Trail and not returning to the town. He backed out of the post office and headed for a service station he had seen on the way to the post office. There, he bought gas and drove the car behind the garage and opened up the trunk. It was then that he noticed Tess's overnight bag in the back of the trunk. In it was some make-up, hose, a dress, hat and some slippers.

What a perfect disguise! If only he had a wig maybe he could pass off as a girl. Where could he find a wig, however, without further jeopardizing his escape. Just then, he noticed that behind the garage was a pasture and a horse sporting a rather long mane. Quickly, he returned to the garage and purchased some tape, several cans of spray paint and scissors. As he returned to the car, he covered the chrome with tape and began to spray paint the top of the sedan, so it rapidly became a two-toned vehicle. He, likewise, took some of the paint and changed a 3 on the license plate to an 8 and a 1 he converted to T. While the paint was drying, he gathered some long green grass growing outside the pasture and enticed the horse to come to him. When he was within arms-length of the horse, he grabbed its halter and used the scissors to trim some of the long dark mane. The horse continued to munch on the fresh grass as Daniel gathered the cuttings and took them over to the trunk. With some of the tape, he attached the strands from the horse's mane in a semicircle inside the hat with several inches dangling down from the brim. He took the hat to the car and put it on his head and looked in the rear-view mirror.

Not too bad! If he was only casually glanced upon, and with some make-up and the dress, maybe he could pass as female. While no one was around, he tried on the dress which was way too short and tight but do-able and climbed in the driver's seat and took off for Trail. As he was heading out of town, he managed to slide on the hose to his knees and placed the slippers just over his toes. At the first stop light, he put on lipstick and some powder as well as tons of eye make-up. As he looked once again into the mirror, he was glad that he had shaved closely that morning and thought he looked a bit like what his father would have called, 'a hussy'.

It was, indeed, his looking like a 'hussy' that called attention to him whenever he stopped to have the service station attendant pump his gas. Intent to not make eye contact nor make conversation, he was subject to cat calls and rude requests. He merely held a ten dollar bill so it covered most of his non-feminine looking hands and pretended to accidently drop it on the pavement.

"Fill it." He would say in his softest voice, as the attendant bent down to pick up the currency. Daniel was hoping the distance and the misdirection of his voice by the car door would perpetuate the ruse. The trip would require three gasoline stops and the first two went reasonably well. As he approached Trail, however, the attendant found Daniel somewhat irresistible and was determined to engage this young beautiful 'hussy' in conversation. Despite numerous head shaking and averting of eye contact, the gas station Romeo just wouldn't quit his amorous intentions. Finally, on the 10-dollar bill, Daniel drew a heart and the telephone number of a rather rough bar that was one of the bank's lending customers. He added, "Ask for Pat". Daniel had worked with Pat, the owner, who was a tough ex-RCAF pilot festooned with tattoos. As he drove off, he blew a fake kiss and wondered what Romeo would think when he called Pat!

The remainder of the trip went as well as could be expected although Daniel wondered what Tess and Gus would think of his new outfit! When he arrived at the hidden driveway he cautiously made his way through the dark to the now newly renovated cabin. As he drew near, he was impressed with the amount of work that must have gone into the framing and hoisting of timbers, joists and tresses creating an almost completely roofed cabin. He knocked loudly on the door and was immediately greeted by Gus and his pistol. As Gus stood aghast at the sight of Daniel in drag, Tess pushed him out of the way and gave Daniel a big hug. That little intimacy brought life back into Daniel's weary soul and body and he answered with a passionate kiss on the lips. Gus beckoned the two back into the cabin from the porch and quickly shut the door.

"How did things go in the big city?" asked Gus.

"I was able to get all of the bills paid but I saw that there was a Wanted Poster with my face on it at the post office. I didn't want to take any chances on the way back. I hope you don't mind having a car with a bit of a different look to it?" Daniel asked with a smile.

"Wow, am I ever impressed with what you have been able to accomplish in just a few days! Show me around the inside. I already know the design talents of your beautiful daughter but am curious how you incorporated the old tree in your design."

Gus showed Daniel around the new addition and was especially proud of the flange he created between the roof line and the old tree. The design allowed the tree to move a bit in the wind but not leak during the torrential rains of the Pacific Northwest. He showed how the tree still maintained its hinged door so in case anyone happened into the cabin, they would not see the opening that led to the mine.

"That looks terrific and no one would notice that the tree was anything but a quirky addition to the cabin's interior. I hope we can get this mine going long before we have to worry about dealing with grandfather's enemies or Mounties looking for me. Now, I'm starving. Is there anything around here to eat?" Daniel's stomach grumbled.

The threesome dined that evening and planned the activities for the next few days. They would work all the next day on getting some gold out of the mine. The following day, Gus would drive the ore to Calgary. The six-hour trip would require an overnight stay but Gus had friends that might expedite the conversion of gold into cash. They might not get as pure a price, but Gus valued caution over squeezing the best deal. Cash was needed for a generator, a pump and less labor intensive equipment.

The following morning the group started down the mine shaft and began the hard work of using a pick and shovel to extract the ore. From the looks of the tailings it might be easier than they contemplated in extracting the rich mineral from the waste. The two men worked with the picks on the mine wall and Tess would take the chunks and use a hand rock hammer to break off the relatively pure gold from the quartz. At the end of the day, they had separated about a bucket of the yellow ore. A bucket weighed nearly 25 kilograms and one kilogram equals 32 troy ounces and, at about $35 per troy ounce, the bucket could bring in over $25,000. Of course, there would be other costs and the need for caution and speed would impact the selling price. They presumed that they might get $20,000 for their day's labor.

The next morning Gus set out for Calgary, leaving Tess and Daniel to work the mine, although they both had other ideas of what the day might provide.

It had been a long time since they had experienced their intimacy in this little cabin, and they both felt a pent-up demand to express their affection for one another. It wasn't long after Gus left that the two revisited the same bed that had shared their bodies' secrets weeks before. This encounter was just as desperate and just as passionate and fulfilling as the first intimacy. The aftermath of the lovemaking presented that warm feeling of well-being and the confidence that comes with the sharing of passion. Both knew that they needed to work the mine or Gus would wonder what they had been engaged in doing instead of working. Still, it was hard to depart from the cozy bed and the touching and kissing that comes with post intimacy.

The couple redoubled their efforts to recover the time spent in personal activities and were able to fill another bucket of reasonably pure ore. That evening brought even more lovemaking and experimentations with other styles of sexual enjoyment. Despite their inexperience, each iteration of their exploration brought even more pleasures. Their discoveries continued well through the evening and into the early part of the morning. When dawn came, the couple was exhausted and no longer concerned about what Gus might think. They were in love and completely committed to each other.

The following day Gus started the long drive back to Trail with the money he had received from his marketing of the gold. He had tried to be careful and discrete, however, gold of such purity would likely cause some eyebrows to be raised. On the return trip he made several changes of direction to throw off any potential interested parties that might be trying to follow him. He was pleased with the amount that the gold brought, and he was anxious to purchase some of the tools that would enhance their life at the cabin and facilitate the extraction of gold from their vein.

At the bank, Mr. Truesdale made a call to Mountie headquarters and spoke with Sargent Bigsby. They agreed to meet in Truesdale's office that afternoon to discuss the situation of the missing cash and Daniel's apparent robbery. Staff at the bank had been whispering as to why Mr. Truesdale didn't seem to be anxious over the missing funds. The fact that he had not assumed an antagonistic posture against Daniel caused some speculation that Mr. Truesdale could be involved, somehow, in the missing funds.

Gus arrived back at the cabin and enlisted Daniel to help him with the heavy equipment back at the car. They now had a generator to run a pump for fresh water and provide electricity for the electric heater and several lamps. Gus had purchased a jack hammer, compressor and a wheelbarrow to increase speed and efficiency at the mine. He explained how he was able to use his contacts for this initial gold but would have to go to the Calgary assayer's office to conduct more volume. That would surely raise suspicions and might require Daniel to accompany Gus on his trips to serve as additional security.

Daniel, thinking of the danger of leaving Tess alone, suggested a different approach.

"Why not enlist the Indian Lone Wolf to ride with you? He has already proven a formidable warrior and could serve as your backup in case of any trouble. I would hate to leave (for a variety of reasons, he thought) Tess up here all alone. Plus, I can't risk being recognized and we could continue to work the mine while you make the trip."

"That sounds like a great plan," Suggested Gus, "I will ride over to the reservation in the morning and see if he is willing. I would have to offer him some explanation, however, and some way of paying him back."

"Gus, as we were working in the tunnel, it occurred to us that the shaft was heading toward reservation land anyhow. It was hard to judge exactly where their territory begins and ends, particularly from underground. Perhaps, after we make a couple of trips to the assayer, we could turn the whole mine over to the Tribe and they could reap some of the rewards that my grandfather intended. With my half Blackfoot blood, I would love to have them be able to finance a library or a school or a medical clinic. The money from the mine could go a long way toward improving their lives," concluded Daniel.

Before going to bed Gus took the cash through the tree and down into the mine. In one of the spurs that had proven worthless he wrapped the cash in a towel and placed it beside a boulder. If anyone were to disturb their sleep, the tree would hide both the mine and their accumulated cash.

Bright and early the following morning Gus once again set off for the trip to the reservation. Since there are no straight streets in the mountains, he guessed the trip might take a couple of hours and another couple of hours in discussions with Lone Wolf and the Tribal Leaders. The thoughts of being alone in the cabin caused Tess to feel some tingling in her spine as she contemplated the intimate delights that the couple had come to appreciate. Daniel had proven to be both gentle and caring but, at the same time, masculine and robust. The combination was more than she had hoped for after hearing the schoolyard gossip of the more 'experienced' girls. They had complained that some guys were either too anxious, too rough or too self-centered to produce a totally satisfying experience.

Daniel, despite his naïveté, had quickly learned to respond to her sounds, motions and breathing. His adaptation to her moods and urges did not diminish his excitement nor his passion. Clearly, the couple recognized that lovemaking was much more important than just the sexual act. And, therefore, they couldn't wait for Gus's departure that morning.

He was barely out of sight when the two embraced, tumbled into bed and made use of the new skills they had acquired. An hour passed as if it was a few minutes and the couple reluctantly started their work down in the mine. With the jackhammer, the work went quickly and the wheelbarrow was quickly filled with ore and pushed toward the hub of the mine's spokes. There the geologist hammers made quick work of separating the gold from the quartz and bucket after bucket was filled before Gus returned from his Pow-wow with Lone Wolf.

"Your Mother and Aunt made quite an impression on the whole tribe and especially with Lone Wolf. I think he would do anything for them and their kin. I explained in simple terms that we needed him to be my bodyguard during trips to Calgary. I told him nothing about the mine or the gold, but he was more than happy to ride in a car and see a big city. Nonetheless, I did mention that, for his services, I would provide his tribe with money to build a school. He was also interested when I said I would supply him with a new Winchester 30-30 and a hunting knife. I will pick him up tomorrow if you have been able to get any gold from the mining today. Did the jackhammer help or was it too difficult to maneuver in the tight spaces of the shaft?"

"I was also able to use the Chief's phone to call your father. He had been visited by the sheriff from Kalispell regarding your whereabouts. The lawman only mentioned that you were wanted in Canada for a felony and, if you happened to show up, give him a call. I explained the whole set of events to your father and he understood. He seemed concerned but had faith that you had good reasons. He said that your mother and Elizabeth were fine."

"Well Dad, why don't you come down and see what we did today?" spoke Tess in her matter-of-fact voice. "We ran out of buckets after the first couple of hours, so we started using jars and pots to bring up the ore."

"Oh, my gosh," exclaimed Gus when he saw the accumulated gold in the bedroom of the cabin. "There must be several hundred thousand dollars of gold there."

"That's what we thought as well. It was so much easier to pull the vein apart from the minerals with the jackhammer. We were able to extract the ore much more quickly with the equipment. I will help you load it in the trunk of the car tomorrow. I just hope the shocks on that car are strong enough to bear all this weight!"

The next morning, with the car all filled with ore, Gus made the trip to pick up Lone Wolf and off to Calgary. On the way, Lone Wolf asked, "Why those rocks so important? They too soft to build anything, too heavy to carry around. I don't understand why white man likes so much."

Gus tried to explain that all through history men of all colors and nationalities have been drawn to gold and its beauty. Gus couldn't think of anything else that gold could be used for other than for jewelry and ornamentation. The rest of the trip they maintained silence.

 The assayer's office was busy when Gus and Lone Wolf came in, each carrying two buckets of ore. Fortunately, Gus had the foresight to place some plain rocks on the top of each bucket to avert suspicions that the near pure gold would engender in the crowded office. The clerk asked Gus to fill out some paperwork while everyone stared at Lone Wolf. Lone Wolf glared back with a presence that signaled, 'Don't even think about messing with me'. The assayer asked the two to enter his office where there could be more privacy. He asked, "Where in the world did you find such gold? I have never seen such a level of purity. I will ascertain its concentration and weight, but will have to give you a check because I don't carry that much cash.

After some haggling, the assayer agreed to provide a check for $350,000. He said that the check would be post-dated until after he had found a buyer for the metal but felt that in just a couple of days the check would clear. Gus asked if the assayer would be interested in more gold if Gus could supply it. The assayer was ecstatic with the prospect and his 'cut' of the product and emphatically indicated he would be more than happy to assist in the marketing of the product.

Gus told him, "If you want to work with us in the future you will have to be completely secretive about this. Hopefully, we can arrange several drop-offs of our findings but, as you know, the walls have ears and we cannot be too careful. In fact, I think that some of the people in your waiting room have already shown some interest in the ore we just brought you."

"Here is what we will do,", responded the assayer. "I will escort you out and express my condolences and ask if you want me to throw out the buckets. I have some old worthless tailings in my back office that I can dump into the parking lot just in case someone doesn't fall for our trick. Let me give you my business card with my phone number. If you have more of this type of delivery, call me ahead of time and I can arrange to meet you after hours or let you in the back door. That way we might avoid any speculation about your frequent appearance in an assayer's office. You are correct in assuming that there are a lot of not-so-good operatives that like to hang around the office."

As Lone Wolf and Gus left the office, they tried to look crestfallen. One of the people waiting in the anteroom smirked at what he presumed were two idiot prospectors whose dreams of riches were dashed. The duo enjoyed a good laugh when they got in the car at the ruse they had over the other prospectors. Gus was pleased to have the check and immediately went to a bank and used it to open an account named Grandfather Mining Company. He thought Daniel would like that as a tribute to the grandfather that he barely knew.

On the return trip to the reservation, the conversation was as sparse as on the ride over. Lone Wolf was silently proud of being selected to carry out this mission and was excited about stopping at a sporting shop to fulfill Gus's promise of a new Winchester and a sharp new knife. At the store on the outskirts of Calgary, they made the purchases and picked up a box of ammunition for both the rifle and the pistol that Elizabeth had loaned Daniel. They were careful not to be monitored nor followed on their way back to the reservation and then home. Lone Wolf agreed to meet up with Gus in a couple of days and they would make a return trip into Calgary.

When Gus returned to the cabin he was pretty well spent from the drama and the day's travels. They all agreed that they need some time off and decided to take a morning break and enjoy a great breakfast together. Gus was not oblivious to the obvious change in the relationship between his daughter and Daniel. It was glaringly apparent that they have affections for one another, and he was just hopeful that the plan they had embarked upon would allow his daughter to continue with the bright life in which they had begun this summer. Without a mother's guidance, he was nervous about how he might assist her in preparation for the changes that were obviously occurring in her life. He was equally concerned about the future of Daniel as he had taken a significant risk in his life and still had a sworn antagonist that was probably, at this moment, tracking them with evil intent.

The next morning, the threesome enjoyed a pancake breakfast with blueberries and crispy bacon. Just the smell of the bacon frying and the coffee percolating gave both energy and optimism to the group that was now considered the Grandfather Mining Company. Gus was, once again, amazed at the amount of gold that Tess and Daniel had extracted and pondered how many times he would need to return to Calgary. He didn't relish the long drive and the concern that he had over carrying large sums of gold to the assayer's office. Even with Lone Wolf's presence, he was nervous over the prospect of someone either cutting him off before he could reach the assayer's office or following him back to his beloved daughter. He worried, more than anything, that she could be in harm's way.

Back at the reservation, Lone Wolf couldn't help but brag a bit about his adventures with the white prospector who was a friend of Lady Elizabeth. In his fireside chatting, he happened to mention that they had carried gold all the way to Calgary. While trying not to be listening, another brave, Tall Tree, was deeply interested in Lone Wolf's meanderings. He was not only jealous of the attention that Lone Wolf had received regarding the two white assassins, but he was also lustful of having a better life off the reservation. With riches, he could do anything and be anyone. With money, he could move to the United States and have a great house with plenty of fancy food and beautiful women. He decided that he would follow Lone Wolf on his next trip and see how he could best benefit from their lucky gold find.

Gus and Lone Wolf made two more trips to Calgary without any particular incident. The assayer was honest and all the checks that he provided them were cleared through the bank so that the account now held a bit over a million and a half dollars. There was still gold in the vein although it had narrowed a bit over the past few days of mining. The trio decided that they would cease any future mining and Gus and Lone Wolf would make one final trip to the assayer's office. They would then turn over the mine to the Blackfoot Nation. Unfortunately, this final excursion might just prove to be catastrophic for the Grandfather Mining Company.

It was predawn Monday morning and Gus, together with Tess and Daniel, drove back to Trail and Elizabeth's little cottage. Knowing that he was a wanted man, Daniel and Tess entered the cabin through the hidden tunnel. They thought it would be safe and could monitor anyone that might be watching the cottage or Elizabeth's house. They would not turn on any lights nor make any sounds that could be heard from outside.

After saying their goodbyes, Gus went to the reservation to pick up Lone Wolf. Only, Lone Wolf was not alone. There, waiting for him was Lone Wolf who was tied up, and the Indian brave Tall Tree.

"What is going on here, Gus inquired, although he partially knew the answer as he quickly produced his pistol. Unfortunately, Tall Tree already had Lone

Wolf's rifle aimed at Gus' head. "Ok, I'll put my gun down but you must release Lone Wolf."

"Lone Wolf will ride with us to Calgary and you will give me the money from the sale of the gold. Only then will you two be allowed to return safely. If either of you tries to stop me in any way the other will die!"

Gus reluctantly drove the two Indians to Calgary with the normal transport of the gold to the assayer's office. Tall Tree had shoved Lone Wolf into the back foot of the vehicle and instructed him to remain silent and not move until they arrived in Calgary. Gus was constantly on edge and concerned that once this new Indian had money, his and Lone Wolf's usefulness would be ended. Or even worse, that he would torture them into revealing the source of the gold. That could put Tess in jeopardy as he was sure that she and Daniel would start searching if they failed to show up at the cottage. The first place they would look would be the mine and that would be where Tall Tree would likely be waiting.

Upon arrival into the back-parking lot of the assayer's office, Tall Tree gagged Lone Wolf and placed Lone Wolf into the trunk of the car. He placed Gus' pistol in his belt behind his jacket and helped carry the buckets of ore to the back door of the office. There he urged Gus through the door and the twosome entered the assayer's office.

The assayer welcomed his clients in and asked them to place the buckets down. He asked, "Gus, what happened to Lone Wolf, I've always enjoyed his tough looks and lack of conversation?"

Before Gus could say anything, Tall Tree interjected, "My tribe mate turned a bit sick so I was asked to be his substitute. We must, however, insist that we get this payment in cash instead of a bank check. The tribe has some needs that can only be satisfied with cash money."

"Well, that seems reasonable if it is OK with you Gus?"

"Yes, it is important that, if you can, pay this shipment in cash if you have it on hand."

"Let me see the weight and the density of the product and I will check to see if I have adequate money's on hand to satisfy payment." Added the assayer who gave Gus a quick knowing look. He had seen much in his day and recognized that this was out of the ordinary and figured that there was more than meets the eye in this transaction.

Gus tried to look nonchalant but there was an edge to his brow as he recognized that the assayer was not fooled by the commentary. He did not wish to have an altercation that might take his, the assayer's or Lone Wolf's life over money. In such, he gave the assayer a brief nod and a smile.

In the meantime, Stone had been hearing rumors of a couple of prospectors, one a tough Indian and the other a strong looking white man that kept showing up at the assayer's office in his home-town. He had been growing increasingly tired of holding up in the hunting lodge in British Columbia and longed for his native Alberta. Stone surmised that, if his father's enemy – the old man that killed his younger brother, was prospecting gold, he was entitled and would find a way to recover his lost riches. As he thought about the Indian, he figured that the Indian must have been from the same reservation that took his two brother's lives. So he was determined to exact his revenge on the two that had virtually wiped out his family and, at the same time, get what was rightfully his!

That Monday, he drove over to the road that led to the reservation. There he waited until a two-toned car sped past and turned into the reservation. He waited and, indeed, the white driver and an Indian headed toward Calgary with the rear end of the vehicle clearly weighted down. Stone followed them all the way into Calgary and to the parking lot of the assayer's office. He waited in an adjacent lot and while he was situating his car, he missed that Lone Wolf had been dumped into the trunk. He only saw the big man and the Indian carrying buckets into the office. He decided he would wait until they came out before acting. If they came out with cash, he would take it. If they had a note, he would kidnap them and force them to take him to the mine. He needed cash now so he hoped that he could simply take that and later find the source of the gold that he felt was his and of his father. He reached into the back seat of the car and grabbed his revolver.

The assayer left the office with the intent of determining the purity of the ore. Instead, he called the local Mounties and asked them to come around. He wasn't sure, but something didn't feel right. In such he felt that caution was most appropriate under the circumstances. He did check to see if he had much cash in his safe. He had nowhere near the amount that would satisfy the purchase of the gold but decided he would offer only a third of the amount that the buckets would be worth. If Gus agreed, then he knew that there was something up, if he balked at the price, then maybe the transaction was legit. In any regard, he put a pistol in his back pocket just as a measure of precaution.

The stack of bills he presented to Gus was impressive, however, Gus recognized that there were a number of smaller bills that were included which gave the stack more credence that necessary. He asked for a receipt and a price per ounce for the deal. The assayer gave him the stack of cash and the bill of sale which Gus immediately recognized as incorrect. He said nothing and the Indian was only focused on the large stack of cash that would change his life. In a surprise to Gus, Tall Tree told the assayer that they would soon be back and would need more cash. At that point Gus realized that this little episode would not be ending well. He or Lone Wolf would be tortured until they provided the source of all this gold. Gus had misjudged the greed that a taste of money can radiate. Tall Tree would not be completely satisfied with this cash that he just stole. He would want much more and probably enslave both he and Lone Wolf to work the mine and transport the ore. That would be a tragedy for Tess and he vowed never to be taken alive. He would fight Tall Tree to the death, if necessary, rather than get back into the car with him.

Stone stepped out of the car just as Gus and the Indian walked out of the office. Stone could see the wad of cash that was now in the hands of the Indian. While he thought that odd, he was blinded in his rage and his lust for the money that was so desperately needed. If he could get his hands on that loot, he could buy his way back into the Calgary illegal establishment. He was certain he could even 'convince' one or the other of them to provide the location of the mine that produced that stack of cash. After all, he was a master of finding ways to make people talk!

Stone walked quickly through the rainy parking lot directly toward the twosome. At the same time, a vehicle carrying two Mounties parked at the assay office and entered the front door. The assayer explained the situation and quickly ushered them to the back door. Stone was within twenty meters before the Indian saw the look on his face and drew his weapon. Stone, likewise, pulled his gun and shot the Indian square in the face. Gus immediately hit the ground just as the Mounties rushed out the back door to witness the murder. Stone trained his gun on the Mounties and they opened fire instantly killing the murder suspect.

Trembling, Gus was interrogated by the Mounties and the assayer verified the legitimacy of his actions. Since Gus had never seen Stone, it took him a while to put two and two together and draw the connection with grandfather's enemies. Hopefully, the final chapter of grandfather's feud had ended. It was only after the interrogation that his thoughts turned to Lone Wolf in the trunk. He asked the Mounties if he could free his associate and they assisted him in releasing Lone Wolf. A bit confused at the sounds he had just heard, Lone Wolf spotted the two bodies and surmised how the events must have unfolded.

With no apparent breach of laws on their part, the Mounties allowed Gus and Lone Wolf to head back to Trail. Before they left, however, the Mounties contacted Superintendent Felps and Sargent Bigsby in their office to apprise them of the recent events. The Trail Mounties had no reason to imply that Gus was anything but a substantial member of the community. They did explain the recent deaths of two brothers at the hands of an Indian named Lone Wolf back on the reservation. The Calgary Mounties suggested that both Gus and Lone Wolf report to the Mounty headquarters in Trail upon their return. Clearly, there were some loose ends that needed to be cleared up.

Meanwhile, when members of the staff entered the bank that Monday morning they were aghast to see Daniel sitting at his new office in the lobby. Mouths dropped even further when Mr. Truesdale entered and shook Daniel's hand as if nothing had happened. However, upon seeing Daniel at the bank, one of the security officers called the Mounties and announced that the bank robber had returned. Unsure of what they might encounter, Felps and Bigsby entered the bank with guns drawn.

"Well, now officers what seems to be the problem today?" asked Mr. Truesdale in his casual and confident tone. The two Mounties looked incredulously at the bank's president and asked if he was okay or was there some sort of hostage situation at the bank. "No problems at all," suggested Mr.

Truesdale, 'we are just celebrating the repayment of one of the largest loans in our history, complete with interest and a prepayment penalty."

"Please explain." Asked Felps.

"Well, our senior loan officer, Daniel, with whom I know you are familiar, made a million-dollar loan to a particular mining company. It was within his responsibility to make such a loan and here is the loan document. He had left the note and its covenants on my desk before he went on a well-deserved vacation. He just returned today and I have ordered a cake for the staff as a celebration. Won't you stay and enjoy a slice of Mrs. O'Brien's special carrot cake? She makes the best pastries in town, you know."

"We thought you had had a robbery when the payroll for the smelter had gone missing."

"I tried to tell you that everything was fine but you went off on this being a federal issue and that we had experienced a robbery. Perhaps you will listen to me next time when I tell you not to pay heed to those that are unaware of the circumstances. Now if you will allow me to make an announcement to my employees as to why you are here and why we are celebrating."

Before leaving, Sargent Bigsby entered Daniel's office and offered his hand.

"I know we have had disagreements in the past and I just want to say that I am sorry and that I hope we can become friends. You have proven to me that, despite you're being a Yank, you are a good man and will be of value to our community."

Daniel was stunned at the relative turn of events but offered his hand to the Sargent.

"I plan on being around here a long time and hope we can develop a friendship. In fact, I would love your help in putting together the legal steps I need to open a clinic and a library on the reservation. My grandfather left me a nice inheritance of cash, but, even more so, he instilled in me that money is not as important as helping others. With your assistance, maybe we can make a difference.

Chapter 12

The wedding took place in Trail that winter in the bleakness that only British Columbia can offer up in late January. Daniel's parents, sister and brother-in-law made the snowy journey up to Canada for the festivities. Mr. and Mr. Truesdale and the entire staff of the bank were in attendance when Gus walked down the aisle with Tess. Sargent Bigsby, who had indeed become a close friend of Daniel served as his 'best man' and Tess' school friends served as bridesmaids. The wedding party was surprised when Elizabeth escorted Lone Wolf down the aisle and sat directly on the front row. He had never before worn a tie or suit and his fidgeting drew some good-natured laughs from the audience.

Daniel had never felt such emotion before. Here he was with new friendships, his family, a great career, his reputation intact and enough money to buy a home for his new bride. He had donated virtually all the remaining money from the mine to establish the Lone Wolf Medical Clinic and the Grandfather Blackfoot Library. He and Tess gave the title of the mine, the cabin and the property to the Blackfoot Tribe, with the stipulation that Gus serve as general manager and his parents and sister receive a combined tenth share of all future proceeds of the mine. He had retained some of the initial returns from the sold gold but was determined to make his future by working hard at the bank. He felt he 'owed' that to Mr. Truesdale who had been his benefactor and mentor. As for Kaak, he remembered his vow when he first met and escorted his great aunt to church for the first time. He donated money to establish an Anglican Church in Kaak, complete with a dedication plaque naming Mr. Truesdale's son as the inspiration for the cathedral.

Tess was splendid when Daniel first saw her walking down aisle toward him. Her dress was exquisite, and her veil and train added to the angelic look that her face always conveyed. His eyes and hers locked and, for a minute, he felt he was back at the cabin when they first made love. It was always her eyes that revealed her soul only to him. That gaze, however, lasted on a few seconds when the tears began to well in his eyes and he became only aware of her presence beside him. He nearly forgot his responses to the preacher as his emotions took hold. Fortunately, Sargent Bigsby gently touched him on the shoulder and brought him back to the ceremony. When the preacher pronounced Daniel and Tess as man and wife, Lone Wolf let out such a holler that it prompted several of the congregation to head for the exits.

At the reception party following the wedding there were the usual alcohol-fueled speeches and testimonials. The powerful presence of Mr.

Truesdale dominated the speeches as he told the stories of Daniel and Tess' first meeting at the diner and Daniel's rather clumsy conversation. Instead of a bride and groom on the top of the wedding cake, there was a log cabin with little gold-colored sugar 'rocks' falling out the door and the windows. Beside the cabin was a tiny facsimile of a tin of 'Gold Dust Tobacco' on the ground. During one of the songs, Tess and Daniel were happy to see Gus 'cutting the rug' with Elizabeth, Daniel's father and mother dancing, and Sarah, her husband and little daughter swaying together to the music. Of considerable interest, however, was Sargent Bigsby who was in a very close encounter with Tess' Maid of Honor. When the two couples were near one another on the dance floor, Tess whispered to Sargent Bigsby, "Do Mounties always get their woman too?"

Biographies

Richard A. Weaver

A native of upstate New York, Richard Weaver is best known as Dick to friends and family. He moved his large family, his wife – Phyllis and six of his seven children to Florida in the early sixties. Working at Cape Canaveral was just one of his many and various jobs, careers and adventures of his life. His latest adventure/challenge is this book. Dick's wife of sixty-eight years says, "He's always looking for another mountain to climb!" The parents of two girls, five boys, grandchildren and great grandchildren, life is never dull here in sunny Florida. It's just an adventure in the making when Mr. Weaver is around. He's always on the lookout for the next new and exciting mountain.

Randy Bateman, CFA

Randy Bateman has been in banking all his career and served as the CEO of several bank subsidiaries and president of a $5 billion mutual fund family. He is an economist by education and currently is the president of Balcones Investment Research where he conducts investment data collection and dissemination through a weekly publication on robotics called <u>The Bot Brief</u>. The newsletter is currently carried on the Robotic Industries Association's website. In the past he has written for or produced information for <u>The LA Times</u>, <u>Boston Globe</u>, <u>Austin American Statesman</u>, <u>Crain's Chicago</u>, <u>Crain's New York</u>, <u>Crain's Detroit</u>, <u>The Miami Herald</u>, <u>The American Banker</u>, <u>Investor's Business Daily</u>, and the <u>San Jose Mercury News</u>. He has been a frequent guest on CNBC, Bloomberg, Fox News, and Jim Cramer's TheStreet.com.